The Baron's Inheritance

A WHISPERING PINES NOVELLA

ROSIE CHAPEL

First printing: 2025
ISBN: 978-1-7637753-6-7 (eBook)
ISBN: 978-1-7637753-7-4 (Paperback)

Ulfire Pty. Ltd.
P.O. Box 1481
South Perth
WA 6951
Australia

www.rosiechapel.com

Cover Design: Rebecca Norman
Images Courtesy: Canva.
Designed in Canva using appropriate licences.

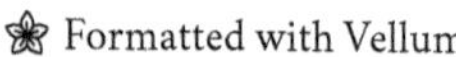 Formatted with Vellum

Acknowledgments

Thank you to…

Mum, Melanie, Jackie, and Brian for your continued support and encouragement.

My hubby for his love, patience, and technical know how.

Graham from Fading Street Publishing Services for fixing my, doubtless, egregious errors.

Perth Rescue Angels, a local charity — without whom we would not have our beautiful Maddie, the inspiration for this story — whose dedication to protecting vulnerable kitties is second to none. Thank you for trusting us with this precious bundle of joy.

Pepsi who makes me laugh every day.

Dedication

To everyone who allows their furkids to rule the house...
...long may it last.

Madam Queen Sorrento (now known as Maddie... but her original name was extremely apt), a rescue cat with a spicy attitude became the inspiration behind Odin, the aristocratic feline featured in this book.

From the day we brought her home (she was not impressed), Maddie's progress, her gradual thaw, and her funny little quirks, contributed to the character of Odin, and I thought you might enjoy a little background.

Three days into this year...2025... we lost our nearly twenty-year-old cat. Neither of us could conceive that within three months, we would be adopting an enormous, mature-aged tabby with the cutest white smudge on her nose, but who was extremely human averse.

We were warned it was unlikely we would ever be able to do more than pat her on the head, and the chance she would allow us to pick her up was negligible.

For a long time, we were greeted with hisses and low growls, but she never showed any aggression, and soon deigned to respond to our tentative advances with slow blinks... a positive sign.

Over the next several months and, exercising far more patience — definitely not my strong suit — than I ever dreamed I possessed, we achieved a minor miracle. Maddie is a different cat. I am able to cuddle her... for longer than two seconds. She loves belly rubs and will let you stroke her all day.

We have a long way to go. She is wary of venturing into the main part of the house and is involved in a battle of wills with Pepsi — our elderly dog and the princess of Rosie Chapeldom — but, even if this is her limit, we are thrilled. The day she sits on my knee, will be the greatest honour.

Maddie

Author's Note

Birthwaite
Prior to the arrival of the Kendal and Windermere Railway
in 1847, the settlement now known as Windermere was
called Birthwaite.

Cumberland
The historic name of the county on the extreme north west
of England, which includes part of the Lake District.
It had an administrative function from the 12th century until
1974 when, along with Westmoreland, it was subsumed into
Cumbria.

Snow Angels
Given the tradition of building snowmen dates back, at least,
to medieval times, it is not a huge stretch of the imagination
to believe snow angels were probably being made long
before the term was recognised formally. A fun and easy
game for all ages: lie on the snow, move your arms up and
down, and your legs in and out and, voilà, there it is — a
shape which resembles a creature with wings.

Although the term *snow angels* was not officially recorded until 1857, one could argue that, for as long as there has been snow, children (and adults) have lain down and waved their limbs to create patterns.

You Will Stay Like That
The phrase pertaining to a person's face freezing in a grimace if the wind changes, or variations thereof, is not formally noted until the mid-C19th. Arguably, given it is part of a wealth of superstitious folklore… meaning its origins are probably much earlier… I employed artistic license.

The Baron's Inheritance

A Whispering Pines Novella

Book One

Chapter One

1819

Autumn

Five enormous coaches crunched to a stop. For a moment nothing happened, even the horses remained motionless as though time was suspended. Then, a flurry of movement as passengers were disgorged, and a melody of voices filled the chill autumnal air.

"My lord." An ever-so slightly travel-crumpled footman opened the door of the first carriage, the one with the coat of arms emblazoned on the side, lowered the step, and bowed.

"Thank you, Craddock." A tall austere-looking gentleman alighted and stretched, his muscles stiff after the interminable journey on less than smooth roads. He breathed in deeply and took stock of his surroundings.

Whispering Pines — a nonsensical name in his opinion, given he could not see a single conifer never mind enough to 'whisper'. He shook his head, aggravation at the farce in which he felt compelled to participate rearing its head.

Lewis Burroughs, the Baron Annersleigh, stared at the

old manor house, unable, quite, to curb the sardonic curl of his lips. The rambling two-storey building appeared to be in a state of disrepair although, at first glance, he surmised the roof was intact… small mercies.

Built from soft, grey stone and embellished with white quoins, the walls were covered in ivy, which would benefit from a good trim as it had all but obscured several of the downstairs windows. From chimneys, dotted across the slate roof like a wonky crown, smoke coiled skywards, drifting into the cloudless blue.

He scanned the grounds, at least, those visible from where he stood. Interestingly, although requiring attention, they did not seem to have suffered unduly from the untimely absence of their last owner, his uncle.

Halstead Thorne, 3rd Marquis of Chesbrough, after being widowed early in his marriage, spent his days here at Whispering Pines, miles from London. He had no children, never remarried, attended parliament with reluctance, and avoided the social whirl of the elite like the plague.

His death, four months previously, at the height of the London Season, had gone unnoticed. It was only when the executor of the marquis' last will and testament called upon Lewis that his extended family — who had not seen Halstead for some years — became aware.

A lonely and rather sad end to a life

Initially, Lewis had ignored the instructions laid out in the will. Approaching thirty years old and a veteran of the recent wars, he was determined no one was going to dictate what he did with the rest of his life, not least an uncle whom he had not seen for over a decade.

It was his mother who persuaded him it was worth the inconvenience. "What is a year to you?" she had asked one afternoon, while the two were taking tea in their vast library, pointing out that, "You are a recluse in the middle of the city, being a recluse in the middle of nowhere ought to suit you perfectly. Go, immerse yourself in the solitude. It is a beautiful area. Read, write your memoirs, walk the estate, learn how to live again."

"Live again? Mama, please, I am not a character in one of your novels."

Thoughtfully, his mother had cupped his chin and held his gaze. "No, you are far too grumpy to be any young lady's idea of a romantic hero. More like the troll who lived under the bridge."

"Mother." His affront obvious.

"Lewis," she echoed in the same tone. "Prove me wrong." The challenge in her shrewd grey eyes did the trick, as she knew it would.

"Fine, you win, but I am only doing this for you." He pushed himself up from his seat and stalked out of the room, a frown marring his rugged features.

His mother allowed herself a small grin of triumph. "Do try to smile, my dear," she called after him. "One day the wind will change, and you shall stay like that."

A grudging chuckle floated back to her as Lewis ran up the stairs two at a time.

Penelope Burroughs, Lady Travers — a veritable repository of old-wives' tales and superstitious sayings — which she recited with ingenuous savoir-faire whenever the mood took her, relaxed in her chair and sipped the fragrant tea.

Discovering Halstead, her only brother, had bequeathed his estate and title to Lewis was not unforeseen as the latter was his sole remaining male relative. That the bequest came with a stipulation was more of a surprise but then, she remembered with a wry smile, Halstead was a staunch advocate of effort equalling appreciation…

...and the reason Lewis ended up in the wilds of Cumberland.

While the handful of staff who had accompanied him from London unloaded the carriages, Lewis strode across the semi-circle of gravel to the great door, in front of which waited five neatly attired, anxious-looking people, otherwise known as his new household... or, at least, a contingent thereof.

Lewis smiled at a gentleman of indeterminate age, dressed in a dark suit, who stepped forwards to greet him.

"Lord Annersleigh." The man bowed respectfully.

"Mr Staples, I presume." Lewis took an educated guess, recalling the information his uncle had left regarding the staff charged with managing the property in the interim.

"The very same, your lordship." The man dipped his head. "I am honoured to welcome you to Whispering Pines. May I introduce Mrs Staples, your housekeeper: Hanson, the foot-man; Lou the maid; and Mrs Coleman, our cook? We thought you might prefer to meet the rest after you have settled in."

"Thank you, Mr Staples, very considerate. I confess the journey although relatively unproblematic was lengthy." Lewis nodded an acknowledgement and exchanged a few words with each of the other four, committing their names to memory.

Mr Staples gave them a moment or two then interjected politely, "Would you like to freshen up before I show you the house?"

"That would be most agreeable." Lewis did not smile as much as his features relaxed marginally, and followed the retainer into the cool interior where he came to an abrupt halt.

His jaw dropped.

The aging exterior belied the beauty within.

The entrance hall was bathed in soft rainbows of light, courtesy of the huge glass dome in the ceiling and the arched, stained-glass window above the front door. The oak staircase, polished to a soft sheen, rose in an elegant sweep to the first floor, where its ornate handrail extended to form a circle around the upstairs gallery.

Lewis spied doors leading off in all directions and was eager to explore, but the notion of a wash and change of clothes outweighed an enthusiasm he had not envisaged.

"If you would be so kind as to come this way, my lord." Mr Staples climbed the stairs and took a right at the top, opening the third door on the left. "Your chambers." He stood to one side, and Lewis stepped into the master suite.

Again, he was astounded by the airiness of his new quarters, which he had expected to be dark and cramped.

Decorated in shades of blue and cream, the palatial bedchamber, with plush four-poster no less, adjoined a dressing room complete with three generous armoires, a private study and, wonder of wonders, a bathing room — a luxury provided by few country estates.

Hugging the corner of the house, meant there were windows aplenty, flooding the rooms with sunlight, and adding warmth to what Lewis perceived was an already comfortable ambience.

"Do you require my assistance…" the butler left his question unfinished.

"Thank you, Mr Staples, I can manage. My luggage?"

"Will be here forthwith." As Mr Staples replied, a knock heralded a fleet of footmen — some from the manor, the rest those who had escorted Lewis from London — conveying a mountain of suitcases.

"Just that one for the moment." Lewis indicated a small valise. "It contains the essentials of life. The others can wait."

"Very good, my lord." Mr Staples nodded at one of the footmen, who hastened to unpack, then, ensuring all was as it ought to be, shepherded the staff out, leaving the new owner of Whispering Pines in peace.

Chapter Two

Lewis crossed to a set of French windows which opened onto a stone balcony. Unlatching them, he stepped out, to be captivated by the view over the estate. From this height it was spectacular and, seemingly, endless.

Trees scattered at random and veiled in the jewel-like shades of the season, looked as though they were floating above the faintest residue of the morning's mist which ghosted the grounds even so late in the day.

Below, a series of lawns, formal and informal, flowed out to the Great Park where, in the distance, he spied a herd of deer gathered near a sprawling copper beech.

His gaze, following a winding track leading from the gardens towards the untamed parkland, caught the sheen of water. A pond, or lake perhaps? He would have to ask.

To his right, the walled kitchen garden, stables, and a collection of outbuildings. Leaning on the balustrade, he saw a group of houses off to the left, probably Home Farm and a couple of the tenants' cottages. Here and there, he spied groups of two or three individuals, presumably going about their daily business.

That was another thing for which he had become responsible: the people who ran this estate. A frown creased his brow. He did not ask for this. What on earth had prompted Uncle Halstead to hang this burden around his neck? While Lewis was not enamoured of the hedonistic lifestyle so loved by his peers, neither did he think he was cut out to run a remote country estate.

Huffing an aggrieved sigh, he turned away from the glorious landscape and applied himself to washing off the dust of the journey.

Stripped to the waist, he strolled into the bedroom, seeking the fresh clothes laid out on the bed by the footman, to be brought up short at the sight of an enormous grey cat, perched atop a chest of drawers, glaring at him through baleful green eyes.

Good afternoon, sir," Lewis essayed, trusting his intuition on the enormity of the creature who appeared to be quite at home in his master's bedchamber.

The cat blinked once… twice… three times, licked one of its front paws with deliberation, then jumped down gracefully, and strutted out for all the world as though he owned the place, tail sticking straight up in the air like a feather duster.

Lewis smothered a bark of laughter at the sheer audacity of the feline. "Now why did you not see fit to warn me about the cat, uncle?" he muttered, drawing a clean shirt over his head. Forgoing a cravat, he bowed to convention by donning a waistcoat and shrugging into a jacket, the latter more for warmth than any other reason.

As Lewis descended the stairs, Mr Staples materialised

from the domestic wing ready to show his new master around.

An hour or so later, his head spinning after exploring the rabbit warren that was now his home, Lewis needed a drink.

"My lord." With the sixth sense inherent to domestic staff, Mr Staples opened a door to the left of the front entrance and ushered his new employer into the library. "Lord Chesbrough liked a brandy of an afternoon." The butler went to a cabinet, tucked discreetly in an alcove. "Happen as you'd be ready for a glass of something after your journey."

"Thank you, Staples, that would be the perfect tonic after a long day." Lewis crossed to the hearth where a fire crackled and popped in the grate. The afternoon was waning. Dusk came early at this time of year, bringing with it the chill of evening.

"At what time do you prefer dinner to be served?" Mr Staples asked, placing a glass containing a healthy measure of brandy on the table by Lewis' elbow.

"What time did my uncle eat?"

"This time o' year, usually about seven. He found dining any later gave him dyspepsia," the butler felt obliged to elaborate.

"Seven is fine, especially tonight. I cannot see myself staying awake much after." Suddenly, Lewis relaxed, a genuine smile warming his face.

"Thank you again, Staples for your gracious welcome. I confess the terms of my uncle's will were unexpected, strange even, but I daresay he had his reasons, oblique though they seem at the moment. Tomorrow, I should like to meet the remainder of the household if you might arrange that for me."

"It will be my pleasure, my lord. Now, you just enjoy your drink. I'll fetch you when dinner is served."

Before Lewis could thank the old retainer again, he was gone, closing the door behind him with a soft click.

Settling into the well-worn, wing-back leather chair, Lewis picked up the glass, swirling the amber liquid which glinted in the glow from the flames leaping in the hearth. Breathing in the subtle aroma of sweet nuttiness with its underlying hint of spice, he took a sip. The spirit slid down his throat with an almost velvety smoothness.

He laid his head on the back of the seat and let his thoughts roam.

As the heat from the fire crept into his tired bones, Lewis was assailed by the inexplicable sensation that he had come home.

Exhaustion, a consequence of the long journey, was not enough to break Lewis' habit, a vestige of army discipline which he could not shake, of waking at first light.

Disoriented, it took a few moments for the cavernous and unfamiliar room, dim in the grey-ish pink of the dawn, to register. Levering himself up onto his elbows, Lewis waited for his brain to catch up with his eyes.

The previous evening, while he dined in solitary splendour, his luggage was unpacked and everything tidied away. When he retired, earlier than normal, the suite had taken on a familiarity unanticipated. His personal effects were arranged exactly how he liked them. His clothes folded into the larger chest of drawers in the same order as in his London bedchamber, and the collection of paraphernalia for his toilette lined up by the bowl in the dressing room.

Deducing Craddock was instrumental in ensuring the chambers were prepared to suit his master, the notion he along with the staff of the manor, were considerate enough to make the new incumbent feel at home was, nevertheless, heartening.

He had slept well… very well. In fact, better than he had slept in longer than he cared to recall. "I was weary from travelling is all," he said to the empty room. The bed was surprisingly comfortable, not too soft that the mattress dipped in the middle, but not too firm that a floorboard would be more appealing.

"Hark at me, ruminating over the attributes of a bed." Lewis threw off the covers and got up, slipping his feet into his favourite pair of slippers, and pulling on a thick woollen banyan.

The embers in the hearth smouldered a dying red. Determined the fire would not go out, Lewis prodded and turned the ashes with the brass poker until they glowed hot, then wedged another log into the grate, watching the flames curl around the wood like grasping fingers. He stood for long moments, basking in the satisfying tendrils of heat, banishing the chilly air.

Crossing to his dressing room, Lewis smothered an unmanly squawk when confronted by the enormous grey cat who was sitting on the window ledge.

Their eyes met and, making a mental note to ask Staples about the creature, Lewis found himself bending a cursory bow at the imperious feline. Still as a statue, the cat stared, unfazed by the interloper in his domain.

"Do you have a name?" Lewis asked before common sense could talk him out of it.

The cat yawned and blinked.

"Am I boring you?" Lewis quizzed. "Gracious, now I am talking to a cat. Assuredly, nigh on ten days confined to a carriage has bamboozled my brain. Are you friendly?" He approached cautiously.

The creature eyed him but did not move.

Lewis extended his arm. The cat sniffed his outstretched hand then gently rubbed his chin along Lewis' fingers which he, gingerly, curled into the soft fur.

So far, so good.

Risking the swipe of a paw, Lewis dared progress from tickling the cat's chin to stroking its head. He was gratified when a quiet rumbling began, which got louder and deeper, and was the most rewarding sound.

"'Tis time I got dressed," he informed the cat. "Mayhap we shall meet again later."

For all the world as though the creature understood, it mewled, hopped down from the ledge and, with a flick of its tail, disappeared.

Startled, Lewis stared. *Where on earth had it gone?* He scoured the corners of the room and checked the windows… no sign of the cat.

Unable to work it out, he gave up.

Sooner or later, they would meet again, of that he was convinced.

Chapter Three

Dressed warmly, Lewis opened the window onto the balcony and sucked in a sharp breath at the crisp air, astonished to see several people already at work in the various gardens.

The sun had breached the horizon, its rays shooting long ribbons of burnished gold through the trees, caressing the earth awake.

From the pearlescent rose of the dawn warming the undersides of the fluffy white clouds, the sky was mired in indecision, morphing through a palette of teal and aquamarine before choosing to paint itself in lapis lazuli.

Like the previous day, a thin mist hovered over a ground sparkling with frost.

It was indescribably beautiful. The gently undulating landscape rolling out to the hills. The twitter of birds stirring, the whisper of voices carried on the breeze.

There was an immutability about the scene, a continuity, as though nothing had changed for decades, centuries even. To be fair, so far from the modern trappings of city life, it was probably true.

. . .

A flash of colour caught his eye, and he looked down at the walled garden. A young woman was weaving among the beds, filling a shallow basket with goodness knows what. Not interested in plants, unable to distinguish a hollyhock from a honeysuckle, Lewis imagined whatever she was picking would adorn the vases, he had spotted around the house, soon enough.

A tune reached his ears; she was singing — with more enthusiasm than virtuosity it must be admitted — but her vaguely off-key rendition was offset by the joy in her voice. The woman was too far away for him to discern her features, except her red hair which glinted like a beacon in the shadowed garden.

Abruptly, the song stopped, and the girl bent down, disappearing behind a stand of tall, leafy plants. She straightened almost immediately but looked misshapen, disconcerting Lewis who blinked in confusion.

Squinting, he tried to figure out what had happened, only to chuckle when a grey, fluffy plume, raised like a flag, flicked back and forth proudly.

The cat.

Indubitably, this creature was lord of the manor, not he.

Shaking his head, Lewis retraced his steps into the bedroom, then made his way downstairs where he was met by Mr Staples.

"Good morning, my lord. I trust you slept well. Breakfast is served in the dining room," the butler greeted with a friendly smile.

Lewis did not question how on earth the man knew he was about to appear at a time the birds scarcely acknowledged, he merely responded in kind. "Thank you, Staples, I slept very well. For all its size, 'tis a cosy room."

"His lordship never complained that is for sure," Mr Staples replied comfortably. "Take a seat, my lord, and Hanson will serve."

"Most appreciated," Lewis said, adding carefully, mindful of the established ways of the household, "After today, might I eat in the study? This is a large room to be heated for one person and, I daresay, I will spend much of my time in either the study or the library. I do not anticipate hosting guests in the near future, if ever, and using rooms for the sake of it seems unnecessary."

Mr Staples opened his mouth to respond, but Lewis got in first. "To be honest, I should be more than happy to eat in the kitchen."

The butler spluttered, "My lord," he expostulated. "I…I…" he dithered, nonplussed.

Lewis grinned and patted the man's shoulder. "Fret not, Staples, I am not trying to offend your sensibilities, but I am just one man." He thought for a moment. "A compromise then. I shall take my meals in the study, allowing us to close the dining room until it is needed, and I promise not to upset the staff by eating in the kitchen."

As he held Mr Staples' gaze, an unspoken message passed between them, reassuring the butler that his new master was not unhinged, simply considerate. Very much like Lord Chesbrough, truth be told.

Mr Staples bowed. "As you wish, my lord."

They shared a smile, then Lewis sat down to a plateful of eggs, ham and toast, washed down with three cups of steaming hot and very tasty coffee. Remote the manor might be but, evidently, its pantry did not lack a rich variety of food.

"Oh, Mr Staples, I almost forgot. How does that enormous grey cat who takes great delight in catching me unawares, fit into this household?"

An agonised expression flitted across the butler's face so fast, Lewis wondered whether he had imagined it. "Begging your pardon, my lord. That is Odin."

"*Odin?*" The fact his uncle had named the feline after a belligerent Norse god, spoke volumes.

"He was gifted to Lord Chesbrough by a friend of the family when he was a kitten."

Lewis waited, sensing there was more.

"He was supposed to be confined to the kitchens to keep the mice at bay, but…" Mr Staples paused, not quite sure how to phrase the slavish adoration Odin had developed for his master which was reciprocated wholeheartedly, not to mention the foot of the bed or the rug by the fire in the library were far more luxurious sleeping quarters than the scullery — rodents aside.

"He preferred the finer things in life?" Lewis, quick on the uptake, finished for him.

Relieved the baron understood, Mr Staples nodded. "He's had the run of the place since then. He is a law unto himself, I'm afraid. Had his lordship wrapped around his paws." Mr Staples did not seem to notice his choice of words. In all likelihood, referring to the cat as though it possessed human characteristics had become second nature. Not unnerving at all.

"Would you like me to get rid of him?" Something in the butler's tone left Lewis in no doubt that his uncle was not the only one at Whispering Pines in Odin's thrall.

"Good heavens, no. Of course not. I only asked because his appearance in the bedchamber came as a surprise. Odin's claim on his domain trumps mine by several whiskers and a tail." Lewis winked at Mr Staples who blew a relieved huff and permitted himself a quick grin.

"Thank you, my lord. I'll see to it he is kept to the domestic quarters."

"Hah, chance will be a fine thing. No, no, do not fret. Let the creature roam at will. I imagine he will do as he chooses regardless. Easier not to restrict him. If the two have been devoted to each other for all these years, the poor creature is probably still expecting uncle to come home at any minute. Animals grieve too you know."

If Mr Staples was the slightest perturbed that his new master sounded as addled as his previous master where animals were concerned, he gave no indication, making do with a bow. "My lord."

"Very good, we are in accord. Please thank Mrs Coleman for a sumptuous breakfast, and I should like to meet the staff…" he glanced at the clock on the mantle, "from ten." He steepled his fingers meditatively. "Perhaps I ought to come to the kitchens, it might be easier than interrupting their day."

Mr Staples curbed his tongue. Clearly, the baron and his uncle were cut from the same cloth. Lord Chesbrough never stood on ceremony unless circumstance dictated and was often seen sitting on a wall smoking his pipe, deep in conversation with one of the gardeners, or leaning against the kitchen doorframe, munching a fresh hunk of bread, or helping muck out the stables. An integral part of the day-to-day running of the estate from within not without.

The notion Lord Annersleigh shared the same attitude warmed the butler who, unaware he was tense, relaxed.

This new chapter in the long life of Whispering Pines was off to a good start — long may it last.

Chapter Four

Ailsa Duval called a bright hello as she entered the quiet hall of the old vicarage, hearing a muffled reply from the direction of the study.

Putting her basket down, she crossed the floor, her boots tapping a tattoo on the cold tiles. Opening a door, she peered around, to see her father bent over his desk, papers and books littering the aged surface.

"Good morning, Papa. Have you eaten yet?" Ailsa gave her father a hug and kissed his whiskery cheek.

"Not yet, my dear, I was waiting for you." Her father returned the hug and smiled at his youngest daughter.

"Shall I ring?"

"Please," he replied absently.

Ailsa's features softened into a loving smile. In matters of theology, Reverend Gervase Duval had a razor-sharp brain. He spoke three archaic languages, knew the bible — several versions — inside out, as well as countless academic tomes. He could quote the most obscure scriptures, and delivered rousing inspirational sermons every Sunday, but when it came to the mundanities of life, such as eating and sleeping, he was wont to forget.

"Come, Papa. I hear Mrs Phelps has cooked up your favourite," Ailsa wheedled.

"Sausage and black pudding?" The vicar raised a bushy brow, shuffling his papers into a reasonably tidy pile.

"With porridge to start."

"Delicious. Best way to start the day. On a full stomach. Nothing beats black pudding you know."

"I know, and I am happy to let you have all of it." Ailsa's nose crinkled in distaste at the very idea of eating fried sheep's blood… her father's meat of choice. Although less common than the typically used pork, the reverend's fondness harked back to when his Scottish wife had introduced the variation early in their marriage.

"Your mama swore by it," Gervase countered. "You do not know what you are missing, my girl."

"We must agree to disagree, Papa." Ailsa gave an exaggerated eye roll and elbowed her father gently. They indulged in the same banter every time black pudding was served.

The pair chatted over breakfast, discussing their respective plans for the day.

"Apparently, the new master has arrived over yonder." Ailsa imparted this snippet of gossip passed on to her by Lou, one of the maids up at the big house, as they sipped their tea. "Lou said it is the Baron Annersleigh. Do you know him?"

"Aye, so I've heard. That'll young Lewis. You remember? Lewis Burroughs who, I believe, is the old marquis' only living male relative. Son of his sister, Penelope. Do you not remember the lad? Mind, he's a few years your senior. Went to war, probably married by now. Hmmm, wonder how he'll find it after all these years."

Gervase rubbed his beard contemplatively. "He was a bit wild when he visited. Dragged you children into scrapes aplenty. Did not seem to come to any harm though, and one form of mischief kept you from another."

"He did?" Ailsa mused, struggling to recall. "I do remember Aunt and Uncle Aumale's visits. Ged and Richard were such fun. Well, Ged really, Richard was a bit stuffy."

"Aumale wanted Richard to understand what it means to be an earl," her father chided gently.

"He was not even ten and four, Papa," Ailsa expostulated. "Had they allowed him to be a boy before forcing him to be an man, mayhap he would not be such an old stick in the mud."

"Ailsa, my dear." Her father was taken aback by her vehemence.

"I shall not apologise. I understand the importance of responsibility, but permitting children to be children is equally essential. If enjoyment, fun, leisure is stripped from one's life, one loses perspective and becomes myopic. 'Tis all about balance you see." Her pearl of wisdom delivered, she sat back.

Amused by her pithy retort, Gervase teased, "When did you become so wise?"

"I have always been wise," she replied loftily, "I prefer not to express it too often for fear of sounding pompous."

"Like you do right now?" he countered archly.

Ailsa pulled a truly gruesome face, and they both laughed.

"Just like your mama." The reverend sighed. "She was never one to reserve her opinion either… should the occasion demand," he added with dry humour.

Ailsa's mother died shortly after Ailsa's birth but — blessed with three older siblings, a devoted father, and caring grandparents — the youngest Duval had not missed what she never knew, although tales of her mother's spirited character were legendary among the family. Ailsa had inherited these traits, along with her mother's red hair — a throwback to her Celtic heritage.

"I wonder what he is like?" Ailsa sought to change the subject.

"Who?" Her father frowned his confusion.

"The new…" she flicked her hand in the general direction of Whispering Pines, "…owner, caretaker, lord of the manor," Ailsa clarified.

"Probably quite the gentleman," Gervase posited. "I daresay Halstead knew what he was doing and considered all the options before making his decision. He would not endow his home to someone he judged an untrustworthy custodian." Giving no hint he was privy to the terms in his late friend's will. Information which would remain confidential, unless circumstances necessitated he reveal his knowledge.

"I struggle to accept he has gone," Ailsa bemoaned. "I thought he would live forever."

"I know, lass, but he was nudging eighty and very tired. I cannot count the number of times he told me he was ready to be reunited with Lady Edith."

"'Tis a long time to be without your wife," Ailsa conceded, then registered her words. "Oh, goodness, forgive me Papa, that was thoughtless."

Her father smiled his understanding and patted her hand across the table. "Do not fret, sweetheart. Life cannot be placed on pause when you lose someone. Hard as it is, you must learn to adjust, to move on.

"Assuredly, had I lingered in grief, your beautiful mother would have descended from heaven to deliver a stern lecture about wallowing. Now, enough of this prattle. My sermon will not write itself. What shall you do today?"

"I thought I might introduce myself to his lordship. Be a good neighbour."

"I suspect you will recognise him when you meet."

"I suspect he will think me a nosy busybody, but we shall see." Ailsa giggled.

"Go on with you, child." Her father rose from the table, squeezed her shoulder as he passed, and returned to his beloved books.

Ailsa lingered for a few more moments then, remembering the flowers she had left in the hall, squawked a muffled oath, and fled. The basket was nowhere to be seen but when she checked in the kitchen, Sarah, one of the maids, affirmed they were in a bucket of water in the scullery.

"Thank you for rescuing them, Sarah. I shall arrange them forthwith." Ailsa beamed at the young girl who grinned in reply.

Collecting the sprays, Alisa spent the next little while replacing the dead stems adorning the assorted vases with fresh flowers. These would be the last of the year. An unseasonably balmy September had coaxed some late blooms, a last gasp of summer, their delicate perfume revitalising the senses.

"There, all done." Ailsa stood back to eye the arrangement. Satisfied, she brushed her palms together. "Perfect, even though I do say so myself. So modest, Ailsa."

She tidied away the mess, then trudged up to her bedchamber where she swapped her well-worn, serviceable grey dress for a much more suitable green gown. Flinging a heavy-knit woollen wrap around her shoulders, she decided to keep her boots on — all the better for tramping across the damp grounds — rather than change them for a pair of shoes, and examined her reflection in the mirror.

Pinning back the odd strand of hair, she studied herself dispassionately.

"You will never catch the eye of a prince," she muttered, "but you might pass muster with a baron."

Chapter Five

Whistling a merry tune, Ailsa followed the rutted lane to the old manor, a path she could walk blindfolded.

For all the day was autumnal, her woollen wrap staving off the cool air, the sun was warm on her face and Ailsa was glad she had forgone the hated bonnet. She carried a parasol as a compromise, but the shaft rested on her shoulders to be, every once in a while, twirled.

The vicarage was a little over a mile from Whispering Pines but, on so lovely a morning, the distance seemed half that.

The manor came into view, and Ailsa stopped as she always did. She loved the old building. The soft grey stone was welcoming and familiar. The gently sloping slate roof with its crooked chimneys redolent of her favourite fairy tales. She probably spent more hours here than she had her own home, certainly of late… until Lord Chesbrough died.

Her earliest memories of the marquis were sitting around the fire with her brother and sisters listening to him read from one of his many tomes. Her father and grandparents, all inveterate bookworms, similarly spellbound.

This was where her love of books started. As she grew older, Uncle Thorne, as he had instructed them to call him, let the siblings read whatever they wanted. From Greek myths and legends to medieval folk tales, to history, art, and religion. His library was eclectic and broad.

Ailsa was the only one whose interest never waned. Her brother, seven years older than she, was more enamoured with outdoor activities, like horse riding and hunting. He went off to war, came home, got married, and moved to Cockermouth.

Neither were her two sisters particularly studious and, as they reached adulthood, lost interest in anything they thought scholarly. Loving though they were, marriage was their goal not learning. Both had made good matches — parenthetically, twin brothers who owned a mill — and now lived near Windermere.

Thus far, Ailsa, despite recently turning the grand old age of two and twenty, had avoided with consummate courtesy, any advances from the local bachelors. She had no desire to get married. She liked her life as it was, unruffled by the demands of a man who cared more for his dogs and his slippers than his wife. To Ailsa, rather than an indignity by which to be humiliated, spinsterhood offered a modicum of independence, something she had no intention of relinquishing.

Recognising Ailsa's thirst for knowledge, Halstead Thorne had approached her father, asking whether the latter had any objections to Ailsa receiving regular, structured lessons, instead of absorbing information at random intervals. Reverend Duval — desirous of his children receiving an education, had taught all of them the basics but had minimal spare time, and the closest school was five miles away — saw no reason to deny the marquis' petition, and so began Ailsa's tuition.

What started as a kindness on the marquis' part morphed into an enduring friendship, which had flourished until four months ago. Ailsa felt the loss of her adopted uncle keenly and was dubious about the arrival of his heir. She could not recall this Lewis Burroughs… mind, it must be over a decade since he had last visited, and people changed, under no illusion he would remember her.

Pushing her memories aside before she became maudlin, Ailsa straightened her spine, metaphorically, and skirted the walled garden, heading for the domestic entrance.

"Good morning, Mrs Coleman," she called to the cook who smiled a greeting and flapped white-coated hands at her.

"Morning, my lovely. Don't get too near, or your dress will end up covered in flour," Mrs Coleman warned.

Ignoring this, Ailsa stretched across the table to kiss the cheery cook's cheek. "Who cares about a bit of flour."

"Go on with you. What brings you here a second time?"

"I thought to introduce myself to the new occupant," Ailsa explained. "Do you know whether it is convenient?"

"Wait you there," Mrs Coleman replied and sent Lou to find Mr Staples. Lou shot Ailsa a knowing grin and hurried out, to return minutes later.

"Mr Staples reckons the master might be amenable to receiving callers. He says for you to pop along, and he will introduce you."

"Might be amenable? Who is this man? His Royal Highness? The Almighty?" Ailsa quipped irreverently.

Lou giggled. "He seems a bit grim if I'm honest," she admitted, "but he only arrived yesterday. Could just be travel weary."

"Don't either of you be hasty in judging the poor man.

Give him a chance. I remember when he came as a lad. Full of mischief he was, but not a nasty bone in his body. You bairns used to spend hours chasing around the grounds." Mrs Coleman nodded at Ailsa. "Lord Chesbrough would not bequeath his beloved home to someone who would not care for it as he did."

"Papa said much the same. I confess, I do not recall him. Perhaps when we meet…" she left that dangling and blew a sigh. "I miss Uncle Thorne is all."

"We all do, lass, but life has to go on. Your uncle would not expect you to mope around. Your ebullience is what kept him going. Now, stop dithering and run along."

"I'll see you on my way out." Ailsa dashed off, hearing the cook's good-humoured *tsk* at her blithe disregard for decorum.

Poking her head into the housekeeper's room tucked in one corner of the Servant's Hall, Ailsa said a quick hello to Mrs Staples, using the time to smooth her dress and ensure her hair was still pinned up. First impressions were important.

Taking care not to burst through the baize door, she crossed the cool hall to where the butler waited outside the library.

"Good morning, Mr Staples," she said, somewhat hesitantly for her. "Do you think me presumptuous calling on Lord Annersleigh when 'tis only his second day in residence?"

Mr Staples' mouth twitched at Ailsa's uncharacteristic reticence. "If 'twas anyone else, yes, but you are as much a part of this house as his lordship. Give me a moment."

The butler knocked and, upon hearing a quiet, "Come," opened the door. A brief and muffled conversation ensued, then Mr Staples returned to usher Ailsa into the room.

"Lord Annersleigh, may I introduce Miss Ailsa Duval?" the butler intoned, then stood aside to admit Ailsa.

Silhouetted against the huge French windows at the far end of the room, a tall man.

Ailsa dipped a curtsy. "Good morning, Lord Annersleigh. I apologise for the early hour, but wanted to extend our… my father's and my… condolences to you, and a welcome."

"Good morning, Miss Duval." His voice was deep and rich, the kind of voice you would never tire of listening to. "Thank you for your consideration, most thoughtful. I have yet to familiarise myself with the estate but am looking forward to it. Would you like to take a seat?" He glanced at the butler. "Mr Staples, might I prevail on you to organise some refreshments?"

"Oh, please do not bother on my account," Ailsa beseeched. "I expect 'tis mere minutes since you finished breakfast." Hearing her words, she clamped her mouth shut and flushed. Her host did not seem perturbed and nodded at the butler who left, the door closing behind him with a soft click.

"If you are sure." Ailsa sank into the closest chair and folded her hands in her lap to stop herself from twiddling her fingers.

"I am always glad to partake of a hot coffee." He paused. "In the same way, I imagine, you are happy to partake of my flowers," his tone bland.

Ailsa's cheeks turned puce. "I-I… b-but how d-did you…? Uncle Th-Thorne… L-Lord Ches… I had permission," she stammered lamely, her voice a mite shrill from an unexpected wave of guilt. The consent had not been granted by the man in front of her.

"From my uncle, I presume? I saw you in the garden this morning," he answered her unfinished question.

She could not read his expression. *Was he angry?* "He

encouraged me to pick them, so they did not go to waste. He said there were always too many flowers for the house. Most of them go into the vases at church," she justified.

He smiled suddenly, and his sombre features relaxed. "Fret not, they are just flowers. You were friends with my uncle?"

"Yes, Lord Chesbrough was a true gentleman, generous with his time and counsel. Papa and he were friends for decades, since both were youths, I think." She sounded stilted even to herself but, unsure of her reception, deemed it wise to behave with formality.

A knock preceded Lou carrying a tray on which stood two tall cups, a coffee pot, jug of cream, bowl of sugar, and a plate of ginger biscuits. She placed it on the table between the chairs and bobbed a curtsy.

"Would you like me to pour, my lord?" she asked.

The baron quirked a brow at Ailsa who, in quick under-standing, nodded.

"Thank you, Lou. I think we can manage. These biscuits smell wonderful, please pass on my appreciation to Mrs Coleman."

That he had committed the names of his staff to memory in so short a time warmed Ailsa's heart. These people were dear to her and, until this moment, she worried about the future of the household, concerned he might be here solely to take an inventory in preparation to sell.

The persistent niggle plaguing her, dissipated.

Chapter Six

Unobtrusively, and inwardly amused by her quick defence with respect to the flowers, Lewis studied the flame-haired young lady, while they sipped their coffee.

Her name rang a very distant bell but her features, arresting though they were, did not, and he presumed they had crossed paths during his almost forgotten childhood.

Their conversation verged on the contrived, and Lewis could not think how to put her at her ease.

After a particularly awkward silence, his guest was the one to break the tension.

"Lord Annersleigh, forgive my boldness, but may I be frank?"

"I should be very glad." He offered a grave smile.

"Papa informs me that, a long time ago, you and I were playmates, of sorts. That when you visited, you joined in our games and fun, became friends with my older siblings, especially my brother, and remain close to my cousins. While I accept this to be true, I must apologise for, to my shame, I do not remember you."

She held his gaze, and her expression tickled at something in his subconscious, gone before he could pin it down. He *did* notice her eyes were the most incredible shade of green, which, along with her hair, hinted at a fiery temper. A vision of her when goaded, not unlike an avenging valkyrie, popped into his head.

Forcing the intriguing, if vaguely discomfiting, image aside, he said, "I too wish I could recall the days of my youth when I had not a care in the world and did not think beyond the moment. Regrettably, they are hazy, perhaps usurped by what went between."

Aware to what he alluded, Ailsa dared pry, "Did you serve?" her tone solicitous.

"It was my honour to do so, but they are not days I care to dwell on, save the comradeship, which survived the atrocities man saw fit to wreak on his fellow man. War is a travesty, and an utter waste of lives to satisfy those who allowed ego to trump reason."

"I cannot disagree." Without thinking, Ailsa stretched across the gap to pat his leg in a comforting gesture, then sought to divert their conversation to a less melancholy topic. "Do you have any plans for the estate?"

He mulled that over. "Not at present. I think it crucial to immerse myself into the daily routine before making any decisions. Wait…" something Ailsa had said came back to him, "…did you say I am friends with your cousins?"

"Yes, Gerard and Richard Mowbray."

"Well, dash it all, I saw them only recently. Both our families attended the nuptials of Nathanial Livingston and Juliette St Clair, last month. A lovely affair," he paused, then added, "I have heard it rumoured that Ged is courting."

"Ged? *Courting?*" Even so far from London and the heady whirl of the elite, Ailsa kept in touch with her relatives, but had yet to learn of this news. "Well, I never thought to see the day."

"It did cause a minor sensation."

"Who is the unlucky lady?" Ailsa's tone was droll, knowing her cousin had long eschewed the bonds of matrimony and assumed this was a match forced upon him by his father.

"'Tis the Earl of Shepperton's daughter."

"Matilda? I heard she was being wooed by the son of a duke."

"No, Melissa." Lewis sat back and waited for the reaction he imagined would follow.

Ailsa did not disappoint.

She gaped at him in slack jawed shock. "Mel*issa?*"

"The very same."

"Surely, you jest? This is not some cruel scheme Ged hatched with Randi? I would not put it past them." The latter being Randolph Craythorpe, Ged's great friend.

"I do not, and Randi was as confounded as the rest of us." Lewis tapped his bottom lip meditatively. "I'll wager there is something afoot, although what I cannot ascertain. That said, to all appearances, on the odd occasion I have seen them together, they seem happy."

"Well." Ailsa shook her head. "Wonders will never cease."

Curiously, the interlude had lowered the invisible barrier the pair had erected. A barrier neither would acknowledge was in place had anyone asked.

Their conversation became light-hearted chatter, and by the end of Ailsa's visit, they had reached a rapport.

"Would you permit me to act as a tour guide?" Ailsa ventured when she stood to take her leave. "I know you will be inundated with offers from any number of the staff but, this way you are likely to get a more… objective answer to your questions or concerns."

"You are an expert on estate management?" Lewis could not help the incredulous curl of his lip.

Ailsa's bright smile wilted, and Lewis could have kicked himself. *No need to be a complete boor,* he admonished inwardly. "My apologies that was uncalled for. I am unused to needing assistance."

Skewering him with a look under which a lesser man would quail, Ailsa did not speak for several seconds, letting the silence stretch out, before replying, "No, not an expert, per se, but Uncle Thorne was a diligent teacher and ensured I learnt more than history and geography. My home may not be as vast as Whispering Pines, but all domiciles require administration of one form or another, if only to keep the pantry stocked."

She spun on her heel. "If you change your mind, Lou knows where I live."

As their burgeoning concord faded, several seemingly unrelated things coalesced into a reasonably coherent picture. For reasons, unbeknownst to him, Lewis did not want to lose the cordiality they had attained.

"Miss Duval, please, my remark was thoughtless. Yes, if you are available, I should be glad of your company. Before you go, might I beg one more moment of your time?"

His contrition was genuine and Ailsa, never one to hold a grudge, turned to face him. "Of course." She inclined her head.

"While my memory is woeful, am I correct in thinking your father is the local vicar? That your mother, for whom you are named, died when you were an infant, and your brother is Lambert Duval with whom I served on the Peninsula?"

The pleasure in Lewis' voice at his sudden recollection was unmistakeable, and Ailsa responded in kind.

"You are absolutely correct. I would not call that woeful at all. You have a better recall than I."

"Mayhap, as you show me around, other details will emerge," he consoled, interested to note that the dread, which usually swamped him at the idea of spending time with someone of the opposite sex, did not materialise.

"What a lovely sentiment, we can but hope." Her sunny smile elicited a corresponding uplift of his spirits. "I am certain you will find great contentment living here. It gets under your skin, becoming so much a part of you that to walk away would be tantamount to severing a limb."

"What does?"

"Everything. The air, the landscape, the house, the people, the weather — yes, even the rain. I promise you."

Her enthusiasm was contagious, but Lewis did not share her optimism. His intention was to stay for one year, to comply with the terms of his uncle's will, then hotfoot it back to London and civility.

He was disconcerted therefore, as he watched the animated countenance of the red-headed woman in front of him extolling the virtues of Whispering Pines and the neighbourhood, to feel his convictions wavering.

Chapter Seven

As Lewis escorted his guest from the library, there was a flash of grey and Odin leapt into Ailsa's arms. She seemed to anticipate the precipitous arrival, her hands steadying the leonine creature who emitted a deep rumble as he butted his head under her chin.

"You have met Odin?" She tilted her head at Lewis who nodded his affirmation.

"He introduced himself to me in my chambers yesterday." Lewis ruffled the cat's great head. Odin stared at his new master and blinked slowly.

"Oh, he likes you?" Ailsa grinned, her fingers buried in the thick fur.

"How on earth can you tell? His customary expression when he sees me seems to be one of resigned indifference."

"Slow blinking," Ailsa replied matter-of-factly.

Lewis had never heard of such a thing. Then again, this was the closest he had ever been to a cat — the entire species of which, to him, were nothing more than vermin eradicators confined to the scullery or stables. "I shall take your word for it." He dared to stroke behind Odin's ears, gratified when the creature pushed its head into his palm.

"See." Ailsa cuddled the cat whose purrs echoed around the quiet hall.

Lewis recalled the butler's comment. "Are you, perchance, the person who presented this beast to my uncle?"

Ailsa met his quizzical gaze over the cat's head. "I am… well, we are. He was a gift from the family. Our cat had a litter of kittens and, given Uncle Thorne had oft complained about the mice in the kitchens, we gave him three. Two, you might be pleased to know, are very happy doing the job they are supposed to do, but Odin preferred the hearth or uncle's knee or even his bed, I believe, to chasing mice. Despite the staff's best efforts, he refused to be constrained. In my opinion, Odin thinks himself master of this house."

"We have met but a handful of times and I cannot refute your assertion." Lewis chuckled. "Even the dogs are in awe of him."

"He certainly comports himself with authority." Ailsa's merriment mingled with that of her host and Odin's loud purring. "I must not interfere with your day any longer. Thank you for your hospitality. I look forward to showing you the estate. "Here…" She deposited the cat into Lewis' surprised hands and, before he could reply, had vanished through the baize door.

Ailsa's generous offer required more than a simple acceptance. It mattered not that the estate was so far from London it might as well have been on the moon, Lewis had no intention of being the reason her virtue was called into question. It was unseemly for an unwed lady to be in the company of a bachelor without the protection of a chaperone.

"No one will notice," Ailsa's breezy reassurance in no way assuaged Lewis' concerns.

The problem was solved, two days later, when the baron called upon Reverend Duval. The vicar trusted his daughter not to conduct herself in an indecorous manner and, as had already been established, anyone Lord Chesbrough regarded as worthy of inheriting Whispering Pines must warrant that same trust, reinforced when the baron gave his word he would behave as a nobleman ought.

Furthermore, as Ailsa took pains to point out, it was too complicated trying to accompany Lord Annersleigh around the estate with a third person. Never mind that the female staff of both houses had enough to do without spending hours traipsing after Ailsa — none of them could ride to save their lives.

The deciding factor was that everyone in the neighbouring hamlet of Chesmere and the smattering of houses surrounding the estate knew everyone else. The slightest hint of impropriety would fly to the ears of the reverend faster than a bullet from a rifle.

For Gervase Duval, who considered himself an astute judge of character and felt a certain kinship with the baron, that was enough.

Thus began an unlikely friendship, or the revival of one long forgotten.

In many respects, Lewis was similar to his uncle. Gentleman both and, as a rule, kind, thoughtful, and considerate of others. Witnessing the horrors of war had left them subdued and somewhat introverted, determined to do whatever necessary to prevent a repeat... despite knowing this was a vain hope. Gallant to a fault, but not without their flaws, or their demons.

Halstead had found solace in his estate, burying himself in the wilds of Cumberland, focusing on creating not destroying, and the reason Whispering Pines was so successful. The herds of deer and cattle, along with flocks of sheep, roaming the Great Park and adjacent fields had thrived under his husbandry, as had the crops. His team of groundsmen were dedicated and knowledgeable. The produce in demand near and far. The beautiful property became a haven — the marquis' personal slice of peace.

Lewis, on the other hand, struggled to adjust to life outside the army. The select few parliamentary committees, of which he was a member, aside — the only diversions were balls, the theatre, and gaming hells. While many returned soldiers embraced such frivolities, the antithesis of war, Lewis found them tedious and headache inducing. He missed the regimented routine and, for a while, floundered.

Perhaps his uncle had the gift of foresight because to administer an estate the size of Whispering Pines would require Lewis to tap into his military discipline yet might also be a place of sanctuary where he could heal.

As she inferred, Ailsa proved a well-informed guide. Determined his adopted niece should be cognisant of the varied responsibilities associated with estate management, Lord Chesbrough was a meticulous teacher and, from the former's familiarity with everyone they met, it was evident she too preferred the hands-on approach.

To Lewis' amazement, instead of the usual aversion he experienced when in the company of women, he found himself in the courtyard, waiting for Ailsa, eager to explore another corner of Whispering Pines. A refreshing, if somewhat unnerving, reaction.

He was not the only one.

Ailsa was similarly enthusiastic but ascribed it to the joy of introducing the baron to her beloved neighbourhood, about which she could wax lyrical for hours.

From their first foray around the estate, what began as a tentative accord strengthened into companionship, even affection — although neither was prepared to admit any such thing.

Days stretched into weeks and, the more they talked, the more memories from childhood were revived. Sundry episodes, thought long forgotten, resurfaced, reducing them to uninhibited mirth. Snatches of a shared past creating an invisible, and as yet unperceived, bond.

As their cordiality evolved from stranger to... dare they presume... friend, one thing became abundantly clear; Ailsa cared not one jot for status or titles, and treated Lewis the way she treated everyone — with good-natured courtesy. While careful not to overstep the bounds of respect, neither did she pander to the baron. If Ailsa did not agree, she said so — usually with vim.

For his part, Lewis relished being able to talk to Ailsa without fear or favour; their relaxed camaraderie reminiscent of that which he once shared with his fellow soldiers. She was intelligent, witty, and eloquent. Whether they were embroiled in a serious discussion, or engaged in light-hearted banter, she could hold her own and never backed down from an argument.

The ladies with whom he brushed shoulders in London tended to fall into three categories. Simpering violets who would not say boo to a goose, haughty young ladies… usually basking in their first season… who expected every man to fall at their feet, or wallflowers more interested in books than the marriage-go-round.

Ailsa was the converse of all three.

There was nothing remotely contrived or affected about this self-possessed young lady who, to Lewis' annoyance, had begun to infiltrate his dreams. Presuming it was because she was the only eligible female within several square miles, he paid no heed.

Neither Ailsa nor Lewis were looking for romance or love. The former did not believe she would meet anyone who came close to the heroes depicted throughout her favourite tomes, while the latter refused to countenance a union arranged for the benefit of others.

A life unencumbered was preferable to a life lacking in devotion.

A philosophy which would, in the not-too-distant future, be put to the test.

Chapter Eight

Almost without realising it, Lewis slotted seamlessly into the gentle rhythm of country life. A routine which adhered to the cycle of the seasons not Society's calendar, and translated into long days in the bracing air, comprehensive meetings with estate stewards or tenant farmers, followed by quiet evenings by the fire.

Exacting, but rewarding.

The change of pace was not the only difference.

Contrary to the the lavish six course, minimum, banquets Lewis once ploughed his way through in London, the fare served at Whispering Pines, although varied and very tasty, was wholesome, limited to two courses and, Lewis realised, far preferable.

Church on Sundays. A practice he never shirked unless unavoidable, yet he found the congregation of the village church… not much bigger than a chapel… to be more devout, more resolute in their faith, and infinitely more welcoming, than that of the church he attended in the city.

He attributed this to the fact that here, in the middle of nowhere, no one cared about *who* you were. The people came for the service — to hear the biblical lessons and learn how interpret those teachings in their everyday lives — *not* to be seen by their peers, flaunting the latest fashions or as a penance for a night at the tables.

The days grew colder and, as November slid into December, the gaudy colours of autumn were subsumed by the monochromatic tones of winter. To an outsider, the vista was harsh, unforgiving, but to the locals it was just a time for hibernation, the slow renewal occurring beneath their feet while the land slept.

Ailsa loved winter. "I feel it is God's way of allowing us to breathe," she explained one day as they rode out to the tenant farms on the periphery of the estate.

"Humph," Lewis grunted, not persuaded. "Too dashed cold for me. I am not enamoured of the grey slush people insist on calling snow, and how it restricts everything. Miserable season, miserable."

"I'll hazard you will change your mind this year," Ailsa contested. "When we get snow, 'tis rarely slushy, never grey, and transforms the countryside into a land of mystery."

"I'll hazard you read too many contes de fées," Lewis snorted. "Land of mystery… bah."

Ailsa giggled at his disgruntled expression. "I shall remind you of this conversation after the first decent blizzard."

"You shall find me huddled under a thick blanket, next to a roaring fire in the library or my study, nursing a large brandy, questioning my sanity."

Ailsa's laughter rang out over the quiet fields. "You are such a city gent," she teased. "Stop equating life here to life in London. While each have their own unique qualities, their individual merits, they are so different that to compare them with such stubborn insistence, leaves you hovering between two worlds."

Lewis twisted in the saddle to watch Ailsa as she spoke, one gloved hand gripping the reins while the other described random arcs in enthusiastic emphasis.

Today, she wore a sage-green riding habit under a form-hugging jacket in a darker shade. In deference to the chill weather, rather than the customary cravat, she had donned a warm knitted scarf, her brother's, she confided, and a pair of lined, leather gloves. Her fiery hair was tucked under a hat in the same hue as her jacket.

At that precise moment, the clouds parted, and a welcome sunbeam illuminated the pair. Ingenuously, Ailsa angled her head to savour the fleeting warmth and, for a split second, was bathed in radiance.

An indeterminate emotion stirred deep within Lewis. Intrigued, he tried to capture it but, as in his dreams, it flitted just out of reach, tormenting him.

The sun was swallowed into the billowing mass gathering above them, casting Ailsa into shadow, and the moment passed.

"Fine, if it satisfies you, I shall reserve my judgment, but do not think you have won this debate." Unable to define, and certainly not prepared to articulate, whatever was ruffling his subconscious, Lewis sought sanctuary in responding to Ailsa's remark.

Ailsa, unaware of his hesitation, clicked the reins of her horse. "Race you," she challenged and was off.

Astonished, Lewis stared after her, then kicked his stallion into a canter. The two hurtled along the tracks and across three fields before slowing to a halt at the edge of one of the farmsteads.

"I won," Ailsa crowed.

"You did have a head start," Lewis retorted as he dismounted.

"Sore loser?" she taunted, an artful gleam in her eye.

Unable to come up with a suitable answer on the spot, Lewis bestowed on her a very childish gesture, making Ailsa chortle all the more.

"Oh, my lord baron, if your London friends could see you now, bested by a vicar's daughter."

"Bah, do not rest on your laurels. We have to get home yet or, mayhap, I shall dunk you in the horse trough and have done."

Ailsa bent over her saddle, helpless with mirth. "Goodness, resorting to dastardly deeds, what would your friends say?"

"That you deserved it."

"For winning?"

"For gloating." Lewis winked and assisted her down.

Their repartee set the tone for the day… and the next several weeks.

For as long as Ailsa could remember, Lord Chesbrough had spent Christmas Day at the vicarage and her father, determined to continue that tradition, invited Lewis.

Initially, the baron felt he ought to decline. He had arrived at Whispering Pines mere weeks ago and, although everyone he met treated him cordially, he remained, essentially, a stranger compared with his uncle. The last thing he wanted was for people to feel obligated to include him in anything, purely because of his connection to the marquis.

After listening to him hemming and hawing, Alisa in her typically forthright manner disabused him of his… in her words, ludicrous sentiment… taking pains to explain the reason he should accept was twofold.

"Firstly, you will be part of a family for the festivities, which is what Christmas is all about. Second, and more importantly, it allows the staff of Whispering Pines to go home."

Seeing confusion crease Lewis' brow, she elucidated, "Uncle Thorne granted his household a day and a half extra holiday from lunchtime on Christmas Day. He maintained that since there was only him, it was unfair to expect them to miss out on being with their families."

"What about his own meals?" Lewis could not imagine a house without a single member of staff.

"He was perfectly capable of filling a plate from the mountain of delicious fare Mrs Coleman never failed to concoct, enough to feed a small army, never mind one marquis and which, I am certain, she will produce again this year.

Lewis was torn. On the one hand, he agreed, on the other he did not share the same relationship with those at the vicarage as had his uncle.

In the end, a frustrated Ailsa, hands on hips, one foot tapping impatiently, implored, "Lord Annersleigh. 'Tis not hard. Stop overthinking and make a decision. Gracious me, are all you noblemen so ambivalent? We are talking about a meal and an afternoon in the company of friends, not whether to invade France. If you are like this in parliamentary committees, it is a wonder our government functions at all."

Lewis smothered a chuckle. "Less of the impudence, Miss Duval. 'Tis not that I do not wish to accept, more—"

"You suppose it to be precipitous given your brief… errr… occupancy to date," Ailsa finished for him.

"In a nutshell, yes." He nodded.

Conscious this could take all day, Ailsa tried a different approach. "I have a little trick which might help. Do you intend to curtail the custom started by your uncle?"

"No," Lewis replied without hesitation.

"Do you wish to spend Christmas Day alone?"

"No."

"Then you have your answer." Her smile was too sweet by half. "We shall expect you at one. Oh, and Odin usually comes too."

"My uncle brought the cat to Christmas lunch?" Lewis was incredulous. *They were all mad, quite mad.*

"Of course. You cannot leave him alone on a day as special as Christmas, he's part of the family." Her cheerful grin left him in no doubt she did not speak in jest.

Chapter Nine

When Lewis awoke two days before Christmas, the light in his room had an unnatural tinge… almost ashen. Unsure whether it was simply the hazy residue of slumber, or the return of the fog which had blanketed the vicinity scant days ago, he pushed back the quilts.

Turning a deaf ear to Odin's mewl of protest at being so rudely awakened — the grey brute had moved from a perfectly decent pile of blankets tucked into an old basket by the hearth, to his master's bed — Lewis dragged himself from the comforting warmth and padded across the carpet to the window.

Neither fog nor the dregs of sleep met his eyes but snow, thick, blindingly white snow. His lips twitched as Ailsa's triumphant exclamation chimed in his head, "Told you so."

He opened the French doors and leant against the jamb, his breath forming little white puffs in the frigid air, which bore a sour edge. Grudgingly, he concurred with Ailsa's assertion. Although dazzlingly beautiful, the familiar vista had been transformed into a land of mystery.

Glistening icicles hung from gnarled and leafless branches coated with rime. The evergreens bordering the lawns looked as though they were cloaked in ermine. Here and there, Lewis spied the outlines of hedges and the dark tracery of wooden fences.

From this belvedere, while there was not a single footprint to mar the wintry landscape, he discerned the pattern of the paths winding their way around the garden beds, and where the lawns became the Great Park. He surmised that, at ground level, if you lost sight of the manor, it would be easy to become disoriented.

Lewis thought back over the past fortnight, which had been wet. Not just moderately damp, but rain of biblical proportions. Torrential downpours had turned tracks to quagmires and roads to rivers.

To his amazement, the routine on the estate continued with barely a hiccup. Seasonal deluges were nothing new to the inhabitants of Cumberland who considered them to be, while occasionally irritating, life-giving in every sense.

The earth was so wet, Lewis could not imagine any snow settling, expecting it to dissolve the instant it touched the land, but the temperatures had plummeted, prompting shepherds to corral the flocks of sheep into their pens and the cows into those fields where stood the protective three-corner sheds. The weatherwise had predicted a cold winter and had prepared in advance.

The snow started falling mid-afternoon the previous day, gently at first then with dizzying ferocity, making any attempt to work or even walk outside impossible. Until the early hours of the morning, a bitter wind had howled around the house, finding its way through even the smallest crack. Mr Staples had ensured the fires, crackling merrily in the grates of all the rooms in use were stoked up throughout the night, and the manor remained relatively snug.

The blizzard had blown itself out… for now… but the sky was laden.

It would be a white Christmas.

One in which, he realised with no small degree of astonishment, he could not wait to participate. It would certainly be different.

A little over a mile away, in the old vicarage, Ailsa was doing much the same as Lewis. In her case, rather than from a stone balcony, she was admiring the scenery from the chicken coop, while she fed the clucking fowl, checked the bedding in their nesting boxes was clean, topped up the waterers, and collected the clutch of eggs laid overnight.

"Brrrr, be glad you have a snug house," she informed the hens who were more interested in what was in her hand than her viewpoint on the cosiness of their abode. "Fine, fine, here you are, you flock of philistines." Her insult failing to register, given they were birds and did not speak human, she grinned and left them to it.

Latching the door, she hurried into the house, careful not to bump the straw-lined pail holding the precious eggs.

She shivered as she entered the kitchen. "Gracious, 'tis cold outside, and I reckon there's more to come, the sky is heavy. If it keeps up like this, we'll be snowed in."

"Aye well, naught we can do about it. We're well stocked up, and Mrs Coleman up at the house says they have plenty to spare if we run short," the unflappable Mrs Phelps assured placidly. "Phelps stacked the wood yesterday, I think we have enough to last until next winter." She chuckled. "I daresay you'll be out there making snowmen before the morning's half over."

"Oh, definitely," Ailsa agreed. It was her favourite winter pastime. Before her siblings moved away, they had competitions to see who could create the most elaborate snowman. Curiously, their father often won, in the main because he had more patience than the rest of them. Even though she was supposed to be an adult, she could not resist indulging in the activity and always persuaded her father into the fun.

"I am out of practice. I wonder whether his majesty up at the Pines will unbend enough to join in?" she mused out loud.

"Don't see why not," Mrs Phelps said, "and stop calling the poor lad his majesty. He's an affable gentleman, for all he's a Londoner. He has accepted the invitation to come here for Christmas luncheon has he not? That suggests he has found his feet and is feeling at home. I thought you two enjoyed each other's company?"

"We do, leastways, on my part. To be fair, he's not as peremptory as I expected him to be..." Ailsa trailed off her gaze turning inward as she recalled the days spent exploring the estate and the neighbourhood.

Before the weather had become too inclement, they had, at Ailsa's behest — her father and a scrumptious picnic in tow — ventured beyond the neighbourhood, to the Borrowdale and Bassenthwaite valley.

"There are plenty of other places, but they are not as close and thus best saved for the warmer months when daylight stretches into the evening," Ailsa explained.

Lewis recalled visiting Derwentwater and Bassenthwaite Lake as a youth, but with maturity came appreciation, especially the long history associated with the region. Inhabited since the neolithic period, in recent centuries, the valley had become a key area for copper and lead mining, in addition to the slate and wool industries.

"One has trouble equating this extraordinary view with the production being undertaken almost beneath our feet," he mused, while they munched on slices of game pie. They had chosen a spot near St Bega's — the tenth century church nestled on the banks of the Bassenthwaite lake under the towering peak of Skiddaw — to eat their lunch.

"It certainly demonstrates a sensitivity for the landscape," Gervase agreed affably, adding drily, "Praise the good Lord."

"I had forgotten all this," Lewis said with some regret as they returned to the manor, making a mental note to see as much as he could when the weather permitted. His declaration that the beauty of the two lakes floating serenely below soaring fells was unsurpassed, endearing him to his listeners.

The more time Ailsa and Lewis spent together, the more relaxed they became, fostered by the hilarity which was induced whenever recollections of childhood romps resurfaced.

Carefree encounters. No hidden agenda. No scrutiny from the sidelines. No expectation beyond the moment.

Ailsa could not deny the erudite and worldly baron was an interesting companion. Not to mention sinfully handsome.

Too frequently for comfort, she found her gaze straying to the kink of his dark hair where it met the collar of his jacket. Too often mesmerised by the flashes of humour in his arresting eyes, the colour of which seemed to lie somewhere between slate grey and lake blue. Invariably, her gaze was drawn to his hands, his efficiency of movement, the muscles which flexed under the fine material of his clothes… not that she was looking.

At night, in the privacy of her room, her mind — never easily quieted — veered off on delectable tangents including how it would feel to be in his embrace, or the sensation of his lips brushing her own, or… the list went on, only to be banished as a nonsensical illusion.

Seeing Ailsa's dreamy expression, Mrs Phelps who had her own opinion, kept her counsel. Hopefully, the pair recognised their latent emotions before intervention proved imperative, or the year was up.

The entire staff of the vicarage and the manor postulated on how well-matched the two were, some even drawing lots on how soon his lordship would declare his suit. That said, the notion, should their suspicions come to fruition, Ailsa might be expected to move to London, tempered their enthusiasm.

Time would tell.

Chapter Ten

Christmas was, in equal amounts, reverent and riotous. Midnight Mass held on Christmas Eve, and the service the following morning were attended by all who were not snowed in. Lewis marvelled at how many had made the effort.

The church — cleaned and polished within an inch of its life, adorned with boughs of fir, holly, and laurel, and lit by innumerable candles — was packed for both services. Locals squeezed into the oak pews and, instead of the usual chatter, a respectful hush descended while they waited for their vicar to deliver the age-old liturgy.

Gervase, who believed a church should resound with uplifting music, always incorporated hymns into his services. This year, he chose The First Noel and God Rest Ye Merry Gentlemen, finishing with Isaac Watts' adapted psalm, Joy to the World. Popular with his congregation, all were sung with gusto, and no one minded the odd wrong note — the bonhomie associated with Christmastide working its customary magic.

"For all their bluff and bluster, the people hereabouts

have a strong faith. Takes more than the odd snow drift to prevent them coming to church," Ailsa said when Lewis voiced his astonishment regarding the packed congregation as they trudged through the hard-packed whiteness to the vicarage where awaited coffee and fruit cake.

After several years' absence, Lambert, Ailsa's brother, and his family had accepted his father's invitation, arriving before the blizzard made travel hazardous. Two became six, the house ringing with the thud of little feet and the revelry of two small children running amok.

No one complained.

Thus, it was seven who sat down to a sumptuous lunch of roast goose with all the trimmings followed by plum pudding. Later, after gifts were exchanged, Gervase, as had Lewis prior to leaving the manor, dispatched any of his staff able to reach their respective homes.

Butler and housekeeper-cook respectively, Mr and Mrs Phelps lived in the cottage adjacent to the vicarage. Although glad to have some private time, the couple had informed their master, in no uncertain terms, he was not to worry about meals, which would be served at their usual time.

Ailsa had tried to argue to no avail.

"Don't you fret about us, lovey." Mrs Phelps had patted the girl's arm in a motherly fashion. "Everything is prepared in advance, just needs serving.

"Which I am capable of doing. There are extra mouths to feed this year, and you both deserve a holiday however short," Ailsa had countered, but Mrs Phelps' mind was made up.

"You think 'tis hard work looking after you pair? I could do it with one hand tied behind my back. It is extra special this year having your brother home, and young Lewis after such a long absence. So, go on with you, let me be." Her twinkling smile persuading Ailsa as little else could.

Once the staff had left or removed next door, and the children, James and Judith, were persuaded upstairs for a nap, the adults retired to the drawing-room where a huge fire blazed. Gervase poured the men a brandy and the women a port.

The minute Lewis was introduced to Lambert, the two recalled their childhood frolics, and had hardly stopped talking since, to Ailsa's well-hidden amusement. Generally, a taciturn sort of gentleman, to hear Lewis chattering like a whole flock of magpies was as unexpected as it was gratifying.

Sipping their port, Alisa and her sister-in-law, Francesca, gossiped about the social whirl of Cockermouth — limited and dissatisfying in Francesca's estimation, but better than nothing.

His duties complete and his stomach full, Gervase snored gently in the comfort of his armchair.

Odin, after reacquainting himself with his siblings in the kitchen and been the willing recipient of too many scraps, had sought Ailsa's lap. His rumbling purr, proof of his utter contentment.

In the middle of her conversation with Francesca, Alisa felt her gaze wander to Lewis, admiring his casual stance as he lounged nonchalantly, one elbow on the mantlepiece and glass in hand, engrossed in a discussion with Lambert about the recent wars and life afterwards.

As though sensing her scrutiny, he turned, and their eyes met. A frisson of something tantalising rippled down Ailsa's spine, and she was unable to prevent the blush which washed up her cheeks at being caught watching him. He smiled, a slow almost lazy smile, and inclined his head. Alisa's heart skipped a beat. She lowered her lashes, ignoring the soft laughter which reached her ears.

When she dared risk another peek, Lewis' attention was focused on Lambert. Unwilling to examine her reaction, Ailsa busied herself fetching the assortment of sweet treats, Mrs Phelps had concocted, then refilled the glasses. By the time she resumed her seat, her equilibrium was restored.

The rest of the day disappeared in a haze of conviviality, enhanced when Ailsa, declaring fresh air to be beneficial after so substantial a feast, coaxed everyone, including Lewis, into the annual snowman competition.

After a few half-hearted, and disregarded, objections, they wrapped up snugly and trudged outside into the crisp afternoon. The sky was cloudless, and a weak sun kept the worst of the chill at bay, but it would not do to stand around.

Gervase gave the signal and, once each had found a suitable corner of the garden, they began.

Predictably, the contest descended into mayhem, especially as the adults had no compunction about sabotaging their rivals' creations. Hilarity abounded and, as the day waned, there was no clear winner, not even Gervase whose snowman suffered an accidental beheading when James fell over Judith during an impromptu snowball fight.

Cheeks rosy, and invigorated by the exercise, they trooped back indoors to be met by steaming hot beakers of hot chocolate, courtesy of Mrs Phelps, and a plate piled with slices of rich ginger cake.

All, feline included, agreed it was a Christmas unsurpassed.

The subsequent days felt — as is always the case after a cheerful gathering, especially Christmastide — rather flat. The snow melted, Lambert and his family left, and the new year was welcomed in almost without notice.

Conscious she had no excuse to extend her association with Lewis, Ailsa was at a loose end — a rare state of affairs. She missed his company, their repartee, their heated debates, and took to riding past the manor in hopes of glimpsing the tall, enigmatic baron, maybe chance a conversation.

Regrettably, if he was abroad, they did not meet.

Had Ailsa but known it, Lewis, for reasons he could not fathom was similarly desirous of perpetuating their acquaintance and, likewise, could not come up with a valid pretext to call upon the vicar's daughter.

Then, during the third week of January, his mother handed him the perfect inducement on a platter... or, more precisely, in a letter.

Owing to the execrable weather, any post was sporadic, so it was a pleasant surprise when Lewis descended the stairs on a blessedly sunny morning to find a neat pile of mail on his desk.

Most were missives pertaining to the estate, along with a couple from colleagues in parliament but one was from his mother. He broke the Travers' seal and unfolded the paper embossed with the family crest.

Two sheets, goodness mama must be bored. He grinned to

himself. His mother bore a healthy antipathy to letter writing and avoided it whenever possible. Using two sheets was unheard of. All he had received from her since his arrival at the manor were three scribbled notes updating him on life in London.

He started to read.

> Dear Lewis,
>
> I hope this finds you well and that you did not feel too isolated at Christmastide. Your absence was noticed at the Hastings' Ball.

Lewis snorted his disbelief. The Duke and Duchess of Hastings' Winter Ball marked the start of the Christmas festivities and, while it was *the* place to be seen, he only went to humour his mother.

He continued. His sister and her family had spent the season at Travers Place, the children — Theresa had three under six years old — were perfect angels. Lewis shook his head, angelic was not the first word that came to mind when describing his nephew and nieces.

He perused the first sheet quickly, somewhat perplexed. His mother, normally succinct to the point of curt, was being uncharacteristically loquacious.

He turned to the second sheet and the puzzle was solved.

> My dear, I yearn to visit you in your new abode. 'Tis many years since I had the pleasure of staying at Whispering Pines and, I believe, a change of scenery will prove the consummate

restorative after the interminably dull weather we have endured. If you are amenable to my proposal, would you have any objections to me bringing two friends? Delightful creatures who never fail to brighten a room.

Lewis' smile morphed into a frown. What was she thinking? Two friends who brighten a room. His stomach knotted. *Please, please do not tell me she is playing matchmaker? Of course, she is. How dare I stand on the cusp of thirty years old and remain unwed? Now I may inherit a title more august than baron, I am considered an attractive prospect. Mother, how could you?*

Silently, he railed at his loving parent. He understood her concerns, but it was his life. If he wanted a wife, he would be married already. There was no shortage of ladies swanning around London Society.

Marriage was not an institution he took lightly. It required dedication, and, if not love, at least an abiding affection. His experiences during the recent wars had scarred him, and, God forbid, should a repeat occur, could not countenance leaving the woman he loved not knowing whether he would return. Worse, any sons born of their union might be catapulted into a future conflict. He knew the fear was irrational but had yet to find a way to overcome it.

Quashing his irritation, Lewis finished the letter, noting… should he be agreeable… Lady Travers hoped to depart London a month hence, allowing him time to respond.

He sat for a long time, mulling over the contents, stroking Odin — who never missed an opportunity to make himself comfortable on his new master's knee — absently.

Well within his rights to refuse her suggestion, using the impediments of travelling at this time of the year, Lewis conceded that made him sound churlish. He huffed an aggrieved sigh, acknowledging he had no plausible justification for denying his mother's request.

Unbidden, as he lifted to pen a reply, Ailsa's face swam across his vision — her impish smile, sparkling green eyes, and flame red hair.

A smile curved his lips... *now* he had reason to call upon her, utterly oblivious as to why this made him so happy.

Chapter Eleven

"You wish me to assist you in orchestrating a house party for your mother and her entourage?" Ailsa wanted to be absolutely clear.

Lewis and she were strolling around the walled garden. Odin, who had deigned to forsake the warmth of the hearth, stalked ahead of them, his great head swinging regally from left to right, eager to rid his territory of unwitting rodents.

"If you would be so kind." Lewis opened his palms in an apologetic gesture. "I have never hosted guests before and, although mama on her own would be no challenge, the ladies accompanying her might expect to be entertained."

They paused, and Ailsa stared at him, a strange emotion gnawing at the notion of ladies… plural… under the same roof as Lewis. Unable to identify it right at that moment, she set it to one side and tried to concentrate. "How many people will be coming?"

"I have no idea. Mama, her two friends and, I presume, a number of staff." Lewis looked like a little boy lost, and it was all Ailsa could do to contain her mirth. Hopeless — men were hopeless. Left to their own devices it was unlikely they would survive a month.

Biting back a grin, she appeared to consider his question with requisite gravity. "I should be glad to guide your endeavours. Have you made a list?"

"A list of what?" Lewis was baffled. *What the deuce have I agreed to?*

"How many rooms must be prepared, for your guests and their retinue. Advise Mrs Coleman of when they are expected and the length of the visit. Menus must be planned in advance to ensure the pantry and larder are stocked with necessities, and that there is enough meat, and fresh vegetables.

"Would you like to have a soiree while they are here? Invite the locals, bearing in mind there are very few titled families in the vicinity—"

"Stop..." Lewis slapped his forehead. "What have I let myself in for?" he lamented. "I thought a few excursions, and a tour of the estate would suffice."

"My lord, a house party provides enough entertainment and activities that guests laud it for weeks. Your table should flaunt the best quality local produce, complemented by the finest wine and spirits. It is the equivalent of the most acclaimed attractions of the London Season, all rolled into one," Ailsa clarified solemnly, picking up Odin and burying her face in his luxurious fur to smother her giggles.

Lewis was aghast. "I cannot match such expectations. I must write to my mother forthwith to cancel. I have neither the patience nor the desire to dance attendance on strangers for the duration."

The abject horror contorting the baron's features was too much for Ailsa who shook with laughter. Odin leapt out of her arms with an offended mewl and vanished into the vegetable patch.

His eyes narrowed. "You are speaking in jest?" he boomed. "You impudent wench."

"Oh, I am s-sorry, but that was too easy. Oh… oh…" Ailsa hugged her sides. "Your face," succumbing to another bout of hilarity.

"You cannot imagine how elated I am to be the source of your levity," Lewis growled.

With difficulty, Ailsa composed herself, but her eyes were brimming with merriment and her smile was mischievous. "You are correct, it does not behove me to provoke. Perhaps that was a trifle exaggerated, nonetheless…" she continued when Lewis looked as though he might interject, "…an occasion of this magnitude is not something to be treated casually. Everything must be organised with exactitude.

"Your household will expand to a substantial number. One cannot improvise on the spur of the moment. Even so far from London, rumours about a disastrous house party will wing their way to salacious scandalmongers waiting to swoop with fiendish glee. Your mother will be the one to bear the brunt of the gossip, not you."

Lewis groaned, "This is a nightmare."

"Come now, you are a baron, in the house of a marquis with a large household to ensure the visit will be a success, and I promise to help," Ailsa mollified. "Between us, we shall arrange a house party worthy of the finest London residences, one not forgotten in a hurry."

Lewis did not look convinced.

Neither had any inkling as to how prophetic Ailsa's blithe assurance would be.

True to her word, Ailsa threw herself into the arrangements with verve, and Whispering Pines became a hive of industry. It was years since the manor had played host to a grand happening… if ever, Lord Chesbrough being somewhat of a recluse… and the staff was determined not to be found lacking.

The house was cleaned and polished within an inch of its life. The pantry and larder were checked and restocked, then menus planned. Suites were aired, beds made up with crisp, fresh linens and thick, down comforters. Fires laid, and huge vases of greenery, liberally besprinkled with painstakingly nurtured blooms from the hothouse, displayed strategically.

Ailsa, uncaring of any family's status, dispatched party invitations to the whole neighbourhood. "Better to include everyone than miss someone," she justified when Lewis gaped at the pile to be delivered. "I daresay some will not be able to come, but is it not said that the more the merrier?" Grinning when Lewis groaned and clutched his head, feigning dismay.

"I prefer not to have one at all, but bow to your recommendation, addled though I think it is. Ouch…" he winced when Ailsa elbowed him in the ribs. "What was the why of that?"

"A warning not to upset the architect of your success." Ailsa wagged a finger. "You asked, I am delivering, now hush and listen."

"Yes, ma'am." He saluted smartly and, with an eye to Alisa's expression, did his utmost to show interest in proceedings. Moved to question whether a whirlwind had taken up residence in the manor, he vanished to the estate office at regular intervals, to be hunted down whenever a decision was needed.

"How should I know?" became his standard response. "Do

whatever you deem appropriate, within the bounds of reason. I do not want this fiasco to bankrupt me."

"Fi*asco*?" Ailsa tutted. "Oh, ye of little faith."

Lewis muttered something unintelligible.

"There, there." She chuckled. "They will be here three days hence, then all you have to do is smile and behave like the gentleman I know you are. Everything else is taken care of, and the fortnight will run like a well-oiled wheel."

"I have a headache, and they have yet to arrive. If 'twas anyone save my mother…"

"Do try not to scowl so fiercely," Ailsa cautioned pertly. "One day the wind will change, and you shall stay like that." Her admonishment, parroting Lady Travers all those months ago, drew a reluctant smile from Lewis.

"On my honour, I will do my best."

"That is all I ask. Now, do you have time to fine-tune the entertainment?"

….and so, it continued, until the crunch of gravel along the curving driveway heralded a fleet of coaches.

Waiting to greet the newcomers, Lewis was beset by the notion this visit would prove pivotal, but for good or bad hung in the balance.

His guests escorted to their respective chambers, with exhortations to join him for drinks once they had freshened up, Lewis retired to the library where he sank into his favourite chair, nursing a large brandy.

While wonderful to see his mother, his verdict regarding the two young ladies remained reserved. Outwardly, they appeared, as professed, delightful. Poised, elegant, and not overly sophisticated… the latter being a trait which grated on

Lewis. Their admiration of the manor seemed genuine, and their conversation, thus far, engaging.

Acknowledging his perspective was coloured by prejudice and cynicism, along with the fact, the new arrivals had been here less than an hour, Lewis resolved to do as Ailsa proposed and embrace the inevitable. Mentally straightening his shoulders, he plastered on a genial smile.

Compared with facing a horde of ruthless French soldiers across a battlefield, entertaining three women ought to be no more onerous than a Sunday afternoon constitutional.

A little over a mile away, in the cosy vicarage parlour, a cup of fragrant tea cooling rapidly on the table beside her and, ostensibly, reading, Ailsa's mind was anywhere but the book on her lap.

For the next fortnight, Lewis' attention would be occupied by two Society ladies who were, doubtless, eminently suitable as prospective brides.

Now, why did that irk her so much?

The first few days of the undesired... on Lewis' part, at least... visit progressed smoothly. Everyone was on their best behaviour and, to be fair, irrespective of Whispering Pines' isolation, the estate was undeniably spectacular, which, along with Ailsa's comprehensive schedule, meant the guests were occupied from breakfast until dinner.

Lewis discovered that Lady Delia Groves and her great friend, as they insisted on reminding everyone, Miss Marianne Fletcher, were known to Lady Travers through their respective mothers. It transpired, Lady Travers' decision to make the journey to Cumberland coincided with the acrimonious termination of Delia's courtship with the Viscount Baudwin.

Delia's mother — who deemed the man a wastrel and only after Delia's considerable dowry — was not upset, but Delia was devastated and felt he had made her an object of ridicule among their peers. Given Delia never went anywhere without Marianne, when Lady Travers suggested a change of scenery might be propitious, she was persuaded to include Miss Fletcher.

Never was Lady Travers so glad to reach her destination. While her two charges were congenial, they were incurable chatterboxes, and the countess' ears were fairly ringing before London had disappeared from sight.

Thankfully, they were travelling with enough carriages that Lewis' mother could plead a headache and retire to one of the other conveyances without appearing rude whenever their gossiping became too much.

It was of some consolation that their voices were melodious for, overnight, Whispering Pines went from restful to rambunctious.

Chapter Twelve

Allowing a couple of days for his guests to recover from their journey, Lewis followed the itinerary, Ailsa and he had devised.

Longer days when they went further afield, were interspersed with horse rides or walks around the estate, and quieter interludes spent painting, sewing, reading, or playing the piano.

The latter were when Lewis could escape for an hour or so claiming estate business.

His mother was not fooled but did not question him. She understood how quickly her son's patience frayed. She *was* intrigued about this Miss Duval whom he mentioned with frequency. Sensing she was more than a passing acquaintance who had helped him arrange the house party, Lady Travers observed the interplay between the two with interest when Ailsa joined them on certain excursions .

The young ladies were charm itself, declaring themselves astonished by the endless views, and the variety of amenities Whispering Pines offered.

Delia's rather snide addendum, "So far from civilisation,"

went unheard by Lewis, but Lady Travers had sharp ears and took note of the murmured slur, hoping it was not a sign of things to come.

Regrettably, it was.

It started when Delia suspected Lord Annersleigh had not the decency to host a ball or any kind of evening soiree in honour of his *esteemed* guests. Pandered to by her parents — who, in the face of her childish tantrums whenever thwarted, found it easier to capitulate than stand firm — Delia expected her every whim to be indulged.

Although in awe of Delia, Marianne the more sensible of the two was not easily influenced by her friend and, for the most part, was the voice of reason curbing Delia's madcap ideas.

Preferring quiet spaces to lavish balls and the hectic whirl of Society events, Marianne rejoiced in the isolation of the manor and its surrounds. The daughter of a viscount, she was not without suitors, but kept all at arm's length, refusing to be rushed into marriage.

Similar to Ailsa, in fact, with whom she felt an affinity the moment they were introduced.

During the previous week, Fortune had favoured the visitors and the milder than seasonal weather held, permitting extended excursions. Sometimes by carriage, occasionally on horseback... picnics packed in saddle bags... Lewis, dragooning Ailsa into acting as guide, had escorted his guests to numerous places of interest.

Not far from the manor, the picturesque little market

town of Keswick, whose soft grey stone and slate buildings seemed to blend into the landscape, hugged the banks of Derwentwater, and presented an eclectic mix of attractions for the discerning visitor.

The market square boasted the recently rebuilt Moot Hall, the original of which, along with the settlement itself, dated back centuries. A browse around the handful of shops, revealed locally made preserves, handicrafts, exquisite linens and wool-wear, even a sweet shop… to the delight of the ladies, and several taverns.

"One can walk right around the lake if one chooses. It is a bit tricky here and there, but the panoramas are glorious," Ailsa explained. "Perhaps a jaunt better saved for the summer months." She grinned at the horrified expression on Delia's face.

Another day, they explored Ambleside at the head of Windermere, which had become a centre for agriculture and the wool trade.

Marianne, as voracious a reader as Ailsa, and always eager to learn as much as she could about everything, had tracked down a publication called *A Guide to the Lakes* by Thomas West, author and antiquary, before she left London. She was overjoyed to see in the flesh, so to speak, some of the attractions featured in the book.

"'Tis wonderful to put a mark against these sites, as a visitor not merely a reader," she had exclaimed when they came upon Bridge House in Ambleside. "Can you credit it… an actual house built into a bridge? Remarkable ingenuity. Although, to wake up each morning hearing water running underneath your bed might be disconcerting." She grimaced comically.

Ailsa's lips twitched . "I am unsure whether it has ever been an abode, perhaps when first built, but now, I believe, it is used to store food."

"Oh, no, how mundane." Marianne's face fell, then brightened. "No." She shook her head resolutely. "I refuse to believe it. In my mind 'tis a cottage worthy of the conte de fees, and no one shall persuade me otherwise," she declared, to the group's amusement.

Her enthusiasm was contagious, and it became something of a challenge to find as many of the places West had chronicled as they were able.

Marianne queried whether they would be able to reach Birthwaite and Bowness on Windermere itself, which were described in the guide and sounded enchanting to the newcomers.

Regrettably, the distance from the manor meant a night at one of the inns would be essential, and something Lewis deemed inadvisable. "A reason to return when daylight lingers into the evenings," he had deflected lightly.

In contrast with Marianne — to whom the wide-open spaces and broad expanses of water were more therapeutic than any tonic supplied by an apothecary — Delia found them intimidating. Her aversion was couched in endless comparisons between the unspoilt serenity of the countryside, and the luxuries London had to offer.

"There is no correlation." Marianne, wearied of Delia's denigration, tried to pour oil on troubled waters. "London's beauty is manmade. It is brick and stone, glass and iron. This…" she swung out her arm to take in the glittering spangles of sunlight dancing on the placid tarn. The patchwork of greens, bronzes, and greys painting the surrounding mountains as they rose in indomitable splendour to kiss the cloudless sky, mirrored in the glassy surface of the lake. The backdrop of gently lapping water, the soft trill of birds, and rustle of leaves in the breeze, "…is nature's architecture and is unsurpassed."

Ailsa stared at the young lady. "Why, Miss Fletcher, I do believe you have the heart of a poet."

Marianne blushed at the compliment, "I certainly understand what inspires them," she replied shyly.

That was two days ago.

"Are you not bored?" Delia wailed as she and Marianne strolled around the formal flowerbeds. The last vestiges of snow had all but melted in the clement temperatures, save tiny pockets of white clinging stubbornly to sheltered corners, supplanted by new growth — hardy, late winter plants daring to push their heads above the protection of the soil.

Here and there, bobbing in the gentle breeze, clumps of snowdrops and crocuses which, along with the soft pastel hues of witch hazel and hellebore, replenished the gardens with a splash of colour, a hint that spring was in the offing. Although cool, the air was fortifying, inviting one to take deep breaths to clear the lungs.

Marianne never wanted to leave.

Given the hectic schedule their host had organised, Marianne was astounded by her friend's peevish and unwarranted complaint. "How on earth have you found time to be bored?" Marianne quizzed. "There is so much to do here. I could walk for miles, or ride out to the boundary of the estate, or even further to one of those magnificent lakes. If you do not wish to be outside, there is plenty to keep one occupied. The collection of books, the instruments. Oh, to paint this landscape."

"Oh pooh." Delia scowled. "You are as tedious as this wretched countryside. Not another soul to be seen for miles.

No one calling. At least Simmington Court is near Bath," referring to her family's country estate. "I expected all manner of activities. Parties galore."

Trying not to feel affronted by the barb, Marianne countered, "Pray, how would you describe the last few days if not full of activities? You do realise we are in the middle of nowhere? Lady Travers explained that there are hardly any neighbours nearby never mind titled families. 'Tis difficult to hold a party when we are the only guests." Swallowing her pique, she instilled a placatory note into her reply.

Delia stamped one well-shod foot. "It is unacceptable." Her mind went off on a tangent. "What do you make of Lord Annersleigh? Do you think him attractive? Perhaps open to a courtship?"

"With you?" Marianne blurted out before she could stop herself. Honestly, Delia was audacious. "My dear, do not assume just because he has been kind enough to open his home to us that he has the faintest interest in anything more… personal. I'll wager he considers us as naught but a temporary distraction."

"*Personal*? Marianne, my dear Marianne, get your head out of the clouds. I do not care about personal. I care about status."

Not for the first time, Marianne wondered why she bothered. "I stand by my assertion. Lord Annersleigh is our host and nothing more."

"Hmmm, we shall see about that."

Exasperated by her friend's stubborn refusal to listen to logic, an imp in Marianne's head prompted her jibe, "Do not expose yourself to more ridicule."

"How could you?"

For once, Marianne was not swayed by Delia's pouting lips and aggrieved tone. "I am simply advocating you not jump in where angels fear to tread. You know nothing of the baron's private life, and with whom he may or may not share it."

Delia's expression hardened into one with which Marianne was familiar. Suppressing a groan, she sought to divert. The last thing she wanted was to wear out their welcome before their sojourn at the manor was half over. Lady Travers did not deserve to have her generosity tarnished by Delia's wilful behaviour.

"Come, the afternoon wanes. Let us seek the hearth. I am sure Lord Annersleigh mentioned tea and cakes. Perhaps a game of chess?"

The notion of sweet treats did the trick, and the pair wandered back to the house, chattering about nothing of any great import.

Marianne sighed with relief, but remained sceptical as to whether Delia would let it lie. The debacle with Lord Baudwin rankled, and Marianne knew her friend was desperate to make a good match, if for no other reason than to rub the reprobate viscount's nose in it.

Lady Travers had let slip that, should her son spend a year at Whispering Pines, he would inherit not only the property in its entirety, but also the Chesbrough marquisate.

While Marianne, a keen observer, surmised the baron had fallen under the spell of the estate and possibly a certain vicar's daughter, unlikely to return to the city unless absolutely essential, she also knew Delia was tenacious when she wanted something. She prayed this was naught but a momentary aberration, and that sanity would prevail before any damage was inflicted.

High above, on the balcony off his quarters, Lewis observed the two ladies unseen. Little did they realise how far voices carried in the stillness.

"So, madam thinks I will fall at her feet, does she? I knew this was a bad idea." A deep frown furrowed his brow as the cogs in his brain began to grind. "How to make it obvious I am not in the market for marriage, without making it obvious.

Odin who was cleaning his paws, canted his head for all the world as though listening. His ears pricked up, then he mewled and pottered back to the warmth of the bedroom.

"If only you could talk." Lewis grinned. "Your counsel would be no less pithy than certain of my parliamentary colleagues."

As the chatter below faded, he closed the door and stood in quiet contemplation. How to fix this? As ever when at a loss, his mind veered to Ailsa. "I wonder…"

Chapter Thirteen

Unexpectedly, despite relishing the excursions with Lewis and his guests, aware the frenetic pace was fleeting, Ailsa realised she missed her solitude. In light of this, she seized the first opportunity to take a constitutional on her own.

Instead of her usual route which skirted the manor, she headed in the opposite direction through Chesmere and beyond towards the hills. Studiously ignoring the fact, this meant she avoided any risk of running into Lady Delia who, for no reason Ailsa could put her finger on, she found enervating.

She rarely encountered anyone on the lonely road and, on a quiet Saturday afternoon there was no one else abroad save the odd fell pony or sheep, which suited her fine. She was not the best company anyway.

"Only ten more days and life will return to normal," she announced to a pheasant foraging in the damp undergrowth who, after a beady-eyed glance, took no notice.

"Ignore me, would you? Think yourself lucky, I am not in the habit of carrying a shotgun and cannot stomach game."

She chortled at her inanity, and continued on her way, enjoying the warmth of the sun on her face — she had forgone a hat, and there was no one around to upbraid her.

The clear blue sky was dotted with wispy clouds reminiscent of ragged cobwebs. High above, a bird of prey wheeled. Tilting her head back and shading her eyes with one hand, Ailsa discerned the distinctive brown and cream plumage of a buzzard's underbelly. Confirmed when she heard the mournful *kee-yaaa* of its call, as it soared on the breeze, either on the hunt for a mate or, and more likely, prey.

She watched it circling, fascinated by the raised v-shape of its wings in flight and the way its tail fanned. Utterly majestic. Suddenly, it swooped in a dramatic dive. Ailsa held her breath. It was one thing to be aware raptors hunted small rodents, quite another to see one catch a poor unwary creature in those vicious talons.

She breathed a sigh of relief when it rose without a meal in its claws. "Wait until I am out of sight," she instructed, and continued on her way. What the eye did not see the heart could not grieve. She walked steadily for another half an hour or so, savouring the peace but when she turned for home, she spotted a rider approaching at some speed.

Unwilling to interrupt his journey — it was definitely a man — she stepped off the track and trod carefully along the grassy wayside. Her attention on the ground to avoid an unladylike trip, rather than on the rider, she was startled by the low, "Whoa," as the horse came to a halt right in front her.

She looked up. It was Lewis.

"Oh," she said, her brain refusing to connect to her mouth.

"Good afternoon, Miss Duval. How convenient."

"It is?" her bemusement plain.

"I was just thinking, I should like to ask your advice and here you are. It is as though Fate read my mind."

"Are you bamming me?" She narrowed her eyes suspiciously.

Lewis clutched his chest theatrically. "You wound me, dear lady. I never, ever bam."

Ailsa giggled. "Yet, you could not have known where to find me… unless…" She quirked a quizzical brow.

"I confess, your father suggested I try this route." He slid off the stallion, patted the creature's neck, and gathered the reins. "Might you permit me to escort you back to the vicarage?"

"I might." Ailsa smiled. "Although, given you are supposed to be entertaining three guests, I sense an ulterior motive. What has happened that you needed to seek me out?"

Unhurriedly, the two set off while Lewis, somewhat diffidently, explained what he had overheard the previous day.

"Ahhh, the lady has set her cap at you?"

"I sincerely hope not, but I fear that may be the case. I am also a trifle irked, she felt moved to disparage my hospitality. As you know, there is a reception arranged for this coming Friday, to include dancing should people so wish. A small affair maybe, but everyone I invited has responded in the affirmative, even your father. While I intended to reveal all at dinner on Wednesday evening, I fear Lady Delia has forced my hand."

"In that case, a pre-emptive strike is called for."

Lewis grinned at her military turn of phrase. "How?"

"Do not give Lady Delia the opportunity to complain. Announce the soiree as a surprise farewell party, that all and sundry are on tenterhooks to meet the visitors from London. That ought to satisfy her." Ailsa could not prevent a hint of sarcasm from creeping into her suggestion.

"Will you come?" Lewis did not realise how much he wanted Ailsa to be there until this moment.

"Of course. I was the one who proposed it, remember," she teased gently. "'Tis not often we get to dress up in all our finery."

"What about...?" Lewis hesitated to enunciate what plagued him.

"Lady Delia's intentions?"

Lewis grimaced. "I know, I sound like a lily-livered ninnyhammer."

Ailsa burst out laughing.

"You seem to find endless humour in my discomfiture," Lewis grumbled.

"Forgive me. Here you are a well-respected soldier, survivor of a brutal conflict, reduced to a dither over a pretty maiden."

"Is she pretty?" he mused over that for a long moment. "I daresay she is considered comely. I had not given it any thought."

Ailsa struggled to decipher why this triggered a burning desire to whoop in a wholly unladylike manner. Making do with a silent cheer, she applied her not inconsiderable intelligence to the problem.

Suggestions were tossed back and forth as they walked until, out of the blue, she had a brainwave. "What say you forestall her advance by alluding to a suit you are already plying?"

"Hmmm... a strategy with merit, but will it suffice? The conversation I overhead... yes, I know what they say about eavesdroppers, but it was not intentional... implied a steely determination. I cannot conjure up a prospective spouse out of thin air." He waved his hand in a kind of flourish, as though wielding a wand, making Ailsa chuckle all the more.

"A well-founded argument indeed and, as an aside, if you

are ever in need of employment, I do believe you would make an impressive street conjuror," she sallied.

Lewis feigned a pained grimace.

Ailsa mustered up her courage. "I do have an idea, but you may regard it as presumptuous."

"I am all ears."

"If, by Friday, it appears your attempts to resist Lady Delia's overtures have failed, I know someone who could be persuaded to become the object of your affection for the evening." Ailsa was trembling at her own temerity, never mind what her father would say if Lewis agreed.

Lewis stopped in the middle of the road and twisted to face her, catching a flicker of something in her astonishing eyes, gone so quickly, he blamed his imagination.

"You do?" A curious air of expectation hung between them.

"I do."

"Am I to be apprised of this paragon's name?"

Ailsa swept a low curtsy. "If it pleases, your lordship, I should be happy to offer my services." She flushed but maintained eye contact, acutely conscious of the fact, despite her father's familial connections, her lack of status might be a stumbling block. "While I may not possess a title, I assure you, I can rise to any occasion when required."

"I have no doubt, and my approbation of a person has never been influenced by their social rank." Involuntarily, Lewis reached out as though to cup her cheek, then realised what he was doing and dropped his hand. He was humbled and, oddly, exhilarated. The notion of a whole evening with Ailsa by his side did peculiar things to his heart rate. Unwilling to explore the reasons for his reaction on the edge of a lonely fell, he pushed it to one side, to be revisited later.

Rather than gushing his appreciation, his reply was a simple, "Thank you, I am in your debt."

"Oh, I am sure I can devise a commensurate settlement," Ailsa replied imperiously, then spoilt it all with a truly diabolical smirk and a sly wink.

"You are a minx." He did not bother to mask his mirth, as he crooked his arm invitingly.

After a brief internal debate, Ailsa accepted, her fingers coming to rest on the fine wool of his riding jacket.

Although neither was prepared to admit it... or even distinguish the underlying cause... the afternoon went from unremarkable to memorable.

Chapter Fourteen

Lewis made the announcement during a sumptuous roast luncheon, after church on Sunday. He had invited Gervase and Ailsa, along with a couple of other local dignitaries and their wives. It made for a jolly meal, and Delia's face when she heard there was to be an *event*… of sorts… was a picture.

Marianne pressed her foot on that of her friend and sent her a meaningful look, at the same moment as Lewis met Ailsa's innocent gaze. The baron bit his lip to prevent an incautious guffaw and, almost smoothly, detailed the form the evening would take.

"A light repast, followed by a musical interlude and, later, dancing. I accept we cannot match the extravagance of a Society ball but, I hope you approve of our efforts."

"I, for one, am looking forward to it." Lady Travers smiled her delight. "I am eager to renew acquaintances, I have not seen in an age."

"As are they." Lewis grinned at his mother. "Squire Tranby especially. Something about a donkey, a fence, and a pond?"

His tone lifted in enquiry, his smile widening when his mother blushed. "Mama?"

"An incident not to be repeated in decent company," Lady Travers replied loftily. "I blame your father."

"Of course you do." Lewis rejoined, then, taking pity on his parent, redirected the conversation.

To the disinterested observer there was nothing noteworthy about the interactions between the luncheon guests, but Lady Travers had discerned a shift in her son's behaviour when in proximity with Miss Ailsa Duval. An appealing notion which bore closer scrutiny.

Later that evening, after Delia and Marianne had retired, Lewis and his mother were in the library partaking of a digestif and a cup of tea, respectively.

"Tell me about Miss Duval," Lady Travers said at a suitable break in their conversation.

Taken aback by so random a question, Lewis recovered with aplomb and prevaricated with studied nonchalance, "There is little to tell, Mama. She has lived next door, so to speak, all her life. Her family were close to Uncle Halstead, and one could be forgiven for thinking she is part of the furniture. Comes and goes as she chooses... at least, she did until recently. Do you know, I spotted her picking flowers the day after I arrived, and she had the nerve to tell me she had permission. Four months after uncle's death. No shame that girl, no shame."

Lewis was unaware his features had softened, and a smile played around his mouth.

Lady Travers held her tongue.

"Apparently, Chesbrough tutored her when she was younger, and they remained great friends. She became, for want of a better descriptor, his companion for years, an adopted niece I suppose, and was devoted to him in his final weeks. Staples informed me she rarely left his side when he was failing."

He recited the overheard conversation and Ailsa's proposal. As he spoke that same tantalising emotion he had experienced the previous day simmered in his subconscious. It was an elusive sensation, almost dreamlike, as though simultaneously flying and falling, but never quite landing.

He missed his mother's speculative glance. "A lady of admirable traits, although, if I may be so bold, she was quite the hoyden as a child. Yes, of course, I remember her. You all played together whenever we visited, despite the age gap among you children. I imagine she has shed some of those tendencies."

Lewis's reply was incomprehensible, somewhere between a chortle and a harrumph.

"Perhaps not quite," Lady Travers paused then added as though barely interested, "and what of your feelings?"

"Mine?" Lewis replied perplexed.

"Yes dear, 'tis plain you harbour an affection for the girl. Is it serious or just a passing fancy?"

Lewis spluttered a contradiction, although it sounded half-hearted at best. "'Tis only for one evening."

His mother gave an unladylike snort and patted his knee. "Lewis, I am not so far into my dotage as to be insensible to my son's moods. Something about this place has wormed its way under your skin, given you a new zest for life. I do not believe it is this house or the estate, or the promise of a marquisate, although I surmise they play a minor role.

"Houses are simply bricks and mortar, estates take a lot of work, and a title is just a title. You are not, have never been, influenced by incidentals. You are not seeking the perfect wife, a lady of status, well-versed in genteel pursuits. You are seeking a partner. One who is intelligent and witty. Prepared to challenge you, to disagree when necessary, but is also fiercely loyal and will love you for you not your title, unconditionally and irrevocably. If I am not mistaken you have found her, but your head is not quite aligned with your heart."

Lewis gaped at his mother. "I-I… b-but… w-when…" he stopped, coerced his brain into some form of coherence, and tried again. "What?" Flinging good manners to the four winds.

"You are in love with Miss Duval. However, because neither of you is interested in courtship, or marriage, neither of you has discerned what is blatantly obvious to everyone else. Except perhaps Lady Delia, upon whom you must keep a sharp eye by the way, she is a manipulative miss. I daresay even Reverend Duval has an inkling. My question is what are you going to do about it?"

So shocked was Lewis by his mother's contention, he was robbed of breath. It was the first time she had spoken to him so candidly. No, not quite true; he recalled her observation after the reading of Chesbrough's will. About to issue a strenuous denial, Lewis thought twice and, staring at the flames leaping in the hearth, pondered her words.

As the silence stretched out, a cornucopia of seemingly inconsequential fragments fell into place and his rebuttal died on his lips. He could no more dismiss his feelings for Ailsa than he could walk on water. Somehow, in a matter of a few short months, without even trying… in fact, he surmised, should he question her on it she would refute the notion with characteristic vigour… she had burrowed her way into his heart, to become indispensable, to become more important than life itself.

The epiphany was both liberating and terrifying.

Well, dammit. What did I say about facing a rabid enemy?

.   .   .

Lady Travers watched a spate of emotions chase across her son's face and permitted herself a small smile of satisfaction. Now, all she had to do was ensure Lewis' sentiment was reciprocated. Not vaguely or tentatively, but with an enduring and indissoluble fervour.

No mean feat, but Lady Travers, expert in the art of interpreting the subtlest nuance, and despite their short acquaintance, had faith in Ailsa.

At the top of the stairs, Lady Travers said. "Would you object to my calling upon Miss Duval?"

"Mama, I beg you not to interfere."

"I? Do afford me some credit, my dear. I think it incumbent that we meet informally prior to Friday. I need her to know I am aware of the plan and support the subterfuge. It will make the supposed courtship between the two of you more plausible if it appears you have my blessing."

Lewis could not argue with her logic. It was imperative Lady Delia believed the match was approved by both families. "Ailsa said she would prime her father, in order that he be persuaded to play along."

"In that case, a meeting of parents would be nothing less than expected, and Ailsa's inclusion on sundry jaunts has already laid the groundwork. If questioned, simply imply that your private life is no one else's business. I recommend you adhere as close to the truth as possible. Less likely to be caught out," his mother advised sagely.

On that note, they said goodnight.

Chapter Fifteen

The next morning, while Lady Delia and Miss Fletcher were still abed, Lewis and his mother took a leisurely stroll to the vicarage.

There was hardly a cloud in the sky and the fresh air was invigorating. Quietly, Lewis prayed the mild weather would continue so as not to delay the departure of his guests a sennight hence.

He loved his mother, but the presence of the two younger women... no, the presence of Lady Delia... was testing his never very tolerant patience.

Her latest complaint, adding to what was fast becoming a litany, targeted Odin. Cats, in her loudly voiced opinion, ought to be confined to the kitchens, better still, the outhouses.

Odin, who *never* lowered himself to associate with the stable cats, seemed to take fiendish glee in tormenting his nemesis. Popping up when she least expected it: in her bedchamber, the library, winding around her legs during meals, and brushing up against her in the dimly lit halls — to her vexed squeals.

Entertainment value aside, Lewis felt it pertinent to point out to the creature that mayhap 'twas was not polite to upset the lady, to which Odin had mewled, stuck his tail in the air, and given his master the cold shoulder for a good thirty minutes... until the warmth of the bedcovers trumped righteous indignation.

"This is pleasant." Lady Travers breathed in the fresh air and linked arms with her son. "By far the best time of the day when so few people are abroad."

"Not the case here, Mama." Lewis smiled. "Most folk are up with the dawn, whatever time of year. There is always much to do."

As though in emphasis, several farmhands appeared, carrying tools and chatting cheerfully amongst themselves.

"My lord." Spotting the baron, they greeted him in unison, tipping their caps respectfully.

Lewis responded in kind and wished them a productive day, with a reminder that, "Mrs Coleman will have hot pies ready at luncheon."

"Aye she never misses a Monday..." one of them grinned, "...and neither do we." The others laughed their agreement.

The group passed and their voices died away.

"I might posit the same happens in London," Lewis went on. "Lamplighters, chimney sweeps, merchants, all manner of people do not have the luxury of sleeping until noon."

"Are you judging me?" Lady Travers arched a finely shaped brow.

"Not at all." He squeezed her arm. "I am merely saying that some of us, myself included, are often ignorant, either by accident or design, of the number of people who beaver away unseen. You cannot deny, the more we have the more we take for granted."

Lady Travers considered this. "Yet, we take great care of our staff."

"Of course you do, as do I, but we tend not to be bothered by things of which we are unaware, and rarely wish to delve deeper, for fear of what we might uncover."

"Goodness, Lewis, this is a profound conversation for a Monday morning."

"Mayhap, but I enjoy frank discussions, and this one has kept us occupied while we walked. See, there is the vicarage." Lewis waved at the building looming up ahead of them.

Built from the same local grey stone as the manor, the vicarage nestled in a substantial garden, encircled by a low wall. Extended over the years, the house with its white framed windows of assorted sizes reflecting the pale winter sky, had rather a whimsical aspect. Across the blue-green slate roof, stocky chimneys topped with clay-fired hoods emitted coils of pine-fragranced smoke, evoking the cottages in folk tales.

"What a lovely home," Lady Travers said as they approached.

"It is as welcoming within," Lewis assured, unlatching the gate and ushering his mother up the path.

Grasping the ornate brass knocker, he rapped sharply and, within seconds, heard a gaily carolled, "Not to worry, Mr Phelps. I am here." The heavy door swung open to reveal a slightly dishevelled Ailsa.

"Oh, good morning, do come in." Automatically, her hands went to her hair, in an attempt to catch the errant strands tumbling out of what had, sometime earlier, been a neat bun. "Forgive my unkemptitude. I am helping Papa rearrange his library and had a disagreement with a ladder and a coal scuttle." Delivered with an insouciance which implied this was not an unusual occurrence.

Lewis pressed his lips together to stifle a smirk. "Miss Duval, I was about to ask whether this might be a suitable moment to discuss errr… Friday with you and the reverend, but perhaps…" he left that dangling.

"Of course, come in, come in. Papa will be thrilled," Ailsa reiterated, showing the pair into the airy parlour. "Please take a seat, I shall be but a moment." She dashed out. "Papa, Papa, we have guests. 'Tis Baron Annersleigh and Lady Travers. Never mind the books, th—" A door banged in the depths of the house, muting her behest.

Reverend Duval appeared; his face wreathed in smiles. "What an unexpected pleasure. How are you?" He encompassed both in his question. "Fine repast yesterday, my lord, my lady. Fine, fine repast. Ailsa…" he frowned, clearly supposing his daughter to be in the room, "…she…"

"…will return momentarily," Lady Travers soothed. "I am savouring my time in Cumberland. 'Tis too long since my last visit. Now Lewis has taken up residence, I hope to travel north more frequently."

"I have not…" Lewis started, to be silenced by his mother's 'do not argue with me' expression.

Just then Ailsa blew back into the room like a miniature gale, followed almost immediately by Mr Phelps bearing a laden tray.

"Thank you, I shall pour." Ailsa smiled at the affable retainer who bowed and, on soundless feet, melted away.

Everyone seated and refreshments served, Ailsa who was no fool, broke the comfortable hush which had descended on the room by asking brightly, "'Tis a joy to welcome you to our humble abode, but to what do we owe this honour?"

Lewis glanced at his mother, whose nod was almost

imperceptible, and clarified the reason for calling at so early an hour.

Gervase Duval's lack of reaction spoke volumes. Evidently, his daughter had enlightened him as to the ruse. He was not entirely convinced. "I am torn between granting my approval and adjuring you not to toy with people's emotions. So many things can go wrong, and I daresay you do not wish poor Lady Delia to leave under a cloud."

"Papa, I have no mind to hurt Lady Delia but, surely, 'tis better to curtail her interest before it manifests? Perhaps over the next few days, Lady Travers might drop a few subtle hints relating to a blossoming courtship between Lord Annersleigh and I. Enough to imply a committed liaison without actually mentioning marriage." Ailsa held her father's troubled gaze. Whatever he read in her eyes swayed him in the affirmative because he dipped his head... albeit grudgingly.

"All I ask is that you are careful. It is a fine line you tread."

"I promise." Ailsa smiled winningly, confident in her acting abilities.

Leaving nothing to chance, the four discussed the minutiae of the evening, ensuring their ploy was not too convoluted.

When Ailsa asked whether anyone would like more coffee, Lady Travers said, "I should be glad of one. Mayhap you and I could have a quiet chat in private while it brews?" In a tone which, while mild, brooked no dissent. "Would you be so kind as to show me your garden?"

The pleading look Lewis sent his mother was ignored with a faint smile.

The two women disappeared, leaving Lewis and Gervase in awkward silence.

Sir..." Lewis felt he ought to elaborate with the vicar. "Might I be blunt?"

Gervase studied Lewis shrewdly. "You might but let us remove to my study."

Chapter Sixteen

Ailsa knew exactly why Lady Travers wanted a word alone. Far from the hedonistic whirl of the elite she might be, but she was no simpleton.

That did not mean she was going to be the one to broach the subject.

Leading the countess along the gravel paths, their cloaks brushing the neatly trimmed box hedge, Ailsa drew her companion's attention to this plant and that shrub. Then, they were through the little wooden gate at the far side of the henhouse, and onto open pasture.

The scenery was no less breathtaking than that from the manor, although here it was left to grow wild in shades of sepia and green. In the distance, the gnarled and denuded woodlands hugging the lower levels of the undulating fells, bled into dark mysterious forests which merged into weather beaten barren peaks, for once, not shrouded in mist.

"I never tire of the view," Ailsa said as, by tacit consent, the two women followed the uneven track towards the village.

"I can imagine. I had forgotten how captivating this area

is," Lady Travers agreed. "My parents brought us here every summer when we were young," she elaborated at Ailsa's inquisitive expression. "I knew your mama," she added gently.

Ailsa glanced at the countess. "I did not," she said matter-of-factly.

"We became friends one summer, shortly after your grandparents moved here. We were close in age, and the only two girls among a group of boys who included us in their riotous games without compunction. To our minds, this was far more fun than learning deportment, or sewing, or any of the other refined pursuits our parents regarded as suitable." Lady Travers' lips curved nostalgically.

"Oh, they were halcyon days, when we had no responsibilities, save worrying whether our clothes would survive our capers. It seems so long ago now," her tone pensive. "We kept in touch even after we both married and my visits to the manor dwindled. I still have her letters, I think.

"Your mother was my first real friend, other than my brother who thought his sibling a pest upon whom he had to keep an eye, in case she fell in the stream, or off a horse, or ate too many apples." Something in Lady Travers' voice made it clear all these things happened with regularity.

An enchanting series of images formed in Ailsa's head, and she felt a stab of grief at missing out on a mother who sounded rather wonderful... if utterly irrepressible. "The only thing I know is that I am named for her."

"You are also very similar to her in looks, and temperament," this last noted with dry humour and Lady Travers went on to share snippets of the older Ailsa Duval, reducing the latter's daughter to helpless giggles.

"She was, if I may be so bold, completely at variance with one's perception of a vicar's wife. Unapologetically unconventional, but a breath of fresh air and no mistake. She was the perfect partner for your father who before he met her was quite the introvert."

"He still is," Ailsa grinned, "except in the pulpit, although he does gain enormous satisfaction from visiting his parishioners," she qualified.

"A quintessential man of God, in fact," Lady Travers observed. "Strong of faith and quiet of deed but not officious, and why his church is always so well-attended." Her perception making her listener's heart glow.

They continued on, making an odd remark about this and that, until Lady Travers asked conversationally, "Do you love my son?"

Ailsa was so startled, she stopped dead. "Beg pardon?" she croaked, praying she had misheard, while frantically trying to formulate an answer.

Lady Travers repeated her question.

"I… errr… I…" Ailsa's brain refused to cooperate with her mouth.

"Forgive my candour, but I believe 'tis my right to ask, especially given the performance in which you pair have decided to engage on Friday evening." While her features were bland, the mild reproof lacing Lady Travers' tone was undeniable.

Ailsa bristled. "Forgive *my* candour, but I do not think 'tis your right at all. Both Lord Annersleigh and I have passed our majority and are quite capable of making our own decisions. Whether they meet with your approval, is not my problem."

"Miss Duval, I do not wish to quarrel, but as a mother I worry," Lady Travers infused a placatory note into her reply.

Ailsa folded her arms and stared at the older woman mulishly. In any other circumstance, her testy expression, reminiscent of Lewis when compelled to listen to unwanted advice, would be comical, but this was not that moment.

Lady Travers sighed. "Perhaps I ought to provide a little background. When Lewis left London, he was in a dark place. His experiences during the wars stole his innocence and stripped him of his natural exuberance. I daresay you recall him as a youth?" She cocked her head at Ailsa who nodded, not quite sure where this was going.

"He smiled all the time, laughter came without thought, and he revelled in bending, sometimes shattering the rules. He was rambunctious, impetuous, and incorrigible. Then he witnessed the atrocities man inflicts on his fellow man in the quest for peace. By the grace of God, he survived, but although his body was unscathed, he was lost within himself, had fallen into a melancholy so deep, I was unsure he would ever recover.

"Then salvation in the form of a bequest. Given your close relationship with my brother, you are, I presume, aware he was a canny soul and always trusted his intuition. Somehow, Halstead knew that endowing his estate to Lewis, would rescue his nephew."

Lady Travers grasped Ailsa's hands and searched her face. "Do you understand what I am trying, maybe not very lucidly, to say?"

"You do not want me to hurt him," Ailsa stated, then raised a palm when Lady Travers opened her mouth to reply, uncaring this was the height of rudeness. "Out of curiosity, how do you suppose one evening pretending to be a courting couple might cause your son irreparable damage? It was arranged to avoid an unkindness. To foil Lady Delia's errr… machinations which might lead to undue embarrassment. It is but one evening." Her brain went off on a tangent.

"Wait, do you suspect *I* have designs on his lordship? That I will lead him a merry dance at the ball? Inveigle him, then cast him aside like last week's broadsheet? What do you take me for, some calculating Jezebel? My lady… gracious… I never did..." Ailsa marched up and down, gesticulating wildly and muttering balefully about people jumping to preposterous conclusions.

Unbidden, Ailsa's outrage struck Lady Travers as funny and, for once, she permitted jocularity to eclipse affront. Her peals of merriment created an unexpected melody with the harsh squawks of a flock of birds flying overhead, the dissonant refrain coming back in silvery echoes.

Ailsa gawked. *What? I must be missing something.*

"Oh, oh, I am sorry, but you..." Unable to control her mirth, Lady Travers succumbed to it. Her hilarity was infectious, and, despite herself, Ailsa joined in. By the time they had regained their composure, the strained atmosphere born of mutual misinterpretation had evaporated.

"Might we start again?" Lady Travers asked when, eventually, she had caught her breath.

"I think it essential." Ailsa grinned. "Preferable to talking at cross purposes."

"Firstly, I am not here to question your motives. Lewis trusts you implicitly and he is no fool. Secondly, although we are little more than strangers, I recognise myself in you. We share certain traits, although I have allowed mine to be diluted over the years, which also means I recognise what prompted your, for want of a better term, escape clause. I'll wager you would jump in a river to save a drowning lamb to your own detriment."

Amusement hovering, Ailsa stifled a giggle at the image of Lewis being compared with drowning lamb.

"Thirdly, I believe the reason for your impassioned reaction is because I hit a nerve, one you are either ignoring or have yet to perceive."

Ailsa stared at the countess, thoroughly perplexed. "What kind of nerve?"

"Corroborating my contention." Lady Travers gave a low

chuckle. "The kind of nerve which requires a person to relinquish control of their reason and embrace their emotions."

"Why must all you Burroughs' speak in riddles," Ailsa lamented, none the wiser.

"Ailsa, I repeat my earlier question. Do you love my son?"

"I-I-I," Ailsa stammered, thinking *even if I did, would it not behove me to tell the object of my affections before I confess all to his mother?*

"Surely it is simple enough. Yes or no?"

"It is *not* simple. Let us, for argument's sake, say I do. What of it? He is a baron. I am a vicar's daughter with no status. Yes, I know," before Lady Travers could interject, "if we are being pedantic, I am related to an earl, but that does not give me a title by association, not to mention I have no dowry. Then there is Papa."

"Which has what to do with anything?" Lady Travers countered, resorting to slang without batting an eyelid.

"I cannot leave him. My siblings live too far away to call upon him routinely. They have families of their own to care for. Papa has only me."

Lady Travers contemplated the younger woman. "That sounds like an excuse, something to hide behind. Do you for one moment suppose your papa wants, nay expects you to forgo a lifetime of happiness to tend to his needs?"

"I am happy," Ailsa argued, stubbornly refusing to grant the grave features of a certain person loitering on the periphery of her consciousness, ascendency.

"Mayhap, but before you consign yourself to spinsterhood, open your heart, just a little. You never know what magic might seduce you."

"Lady Travers... I... you ... *magic?*" Ailsa squeaked.

"I may be a very important countess now..." Lady Travers' regal tone at odds with the wicked glint in her blue-grey eyes — so similar to her son's it was uncanny, "...but I was young once. While fortunate to have married for love, it was not the union my parents selected. Persuading them it was Alfred or no one was akin to battling an implacable foe. The duke they preferred was two decades older and, quite frankly, less attractive than a toad, but a duke nonetheless."

Ailsa felt a tug on her heartstrings at the predicament Lady Travers had overcome. It took fortitude to defy your parents.

"Eventually, I informed them, I would enter a convent rather than marry their deplorable choice. Thankfully, they yielded."

"Very courageous, but…"

"Sometimes one has to reach for the dream, Ailsa. Your plan offers the perfect opportunity, and better to take the risk now before it's too late."

"Too late? How can it be too late? Lewis has been here scant months." Ailsa frowned her incomprehension.

"You do know about the will?"

"That Lewis inherited the estate."

"He has not elaborated…"

"What reason has he to divulge the terms of Uncle Thorne's will? It is a private matter. I am…"

This time it was Lady Travers' hand which went up. "Do not say it. Gracious, my girl, status is not all about titles, as I said to my son yesterday." She drew a long-suffering sigh. "Ailsa, Lewis only has to stay at Whispering Pines for a year to inherit the marquisate. I do not know what he intends to do once the twelve months is over."

There was a shocked silence.

The colour drained from Ailsa's face as fast as her smile.

Aghast, she backed away, shaking her head. "Only a year? One year? All this was for a bloody *title*? Ohhhhhhh…" she turned on her heel and fled.

Chapter Seventeen

Ailsa slammed into the vicarage yelling, "Lord Annersleigh, get your grumpiness out here this instant."

No response.

"I know you are still here. You and I are due a quiet chat."

A rumble of conversation drifted to her from the study, then the door opened, and two faces peered out, bearing matching expressions of stupefaction.

"Papa, forgive the interruption, but I must speak with his lordship." The smile Ailsa bestowed on her father was alarmingly sweet.

Gervase pressed his lips together and muttered, "Best not tarry. I know that look."

Lewis crossed the hall to where Ailsa waited foot tapping. "Miss Duval? What has caused such disquiet? My mother…"

"Expounded on certain aspects of your sojourn here in Cumberland. Walk with me, would you?"

Lewis glanced over his shoulder at Gervase who shrugged and nodded in tacit indication that the baron's continued health relied on doing as Ailsa had bidden.

Wordlessly, while scouring his brain as to what the devil had caused Ailsa's abrupt change of mood, Lewis followed her out of the front door, through the garden, and onto the lane leading to the manor.

They walked without speaking until out of earshot of the vicarage, then Ailsa, face like thunder, stopped and turned to confront Lewis.

"I wonder, my lord, when were you going to tell me?"

"Tell you what?" Lewis' bafflement was patent.

"The reason you are here."

"To assume ownership of the property my uncle endowed upon me."

"Ahhh, this we all know, but you left out the most important part."

"Enlighten me." Deep lines furrowed Lewis' forehead.

"The terms! A year. If you stay here for a year, all this becomes yours and your descendants in perpetuity, along with the marquisate."

"You did not know?" That the shock on Lewis' face was genuine, came as no solace to Ailsa.

"Do I sound like someone acquainted with all the salient details? Do people in the know make a habit of upbraiding the source of those facts, or lack thereof, in the middle of a path," Ailsa snapped sarcastically.

"Ailsa, forgive me, I thought everyone here was aware of the terms, long before the lawyer tracked me down. I supposed my uncle had informed all those closest to him before his death, especially his household, to forestall the inevitable consternation any change would cause. Your own father was one of the witnesses to the will. I am astonished he did not tell you."

"Obviously, had anyone thought it pertinent to apprise me, we would not be having this discussion and, I presume,

Papa deemed the contents confidential," she huffed. "Then you arrive, you seem to settle in, I offer to be your tour guide, drag you around the estate…"

"I do not think I was dragged." Lewis tried to infuse some levity into their conversation.

Ailsa carried on as though he had not spoken, "…spend hours with you talking about everything from how estates are run, to shared childhood memories, to… to… life in general. Not once, in all those encounters did you mention that when summer is over you will leave." She threw up her hands in frustration.

Lewis tried to interject, but Ailsa had worked herself up into a fine old tantrum and, her muddled, somewhat irrational, allegation aside was not interested in his platitudes. Neither had she connected that Lady Travers' hypothesis, and her own indignation stemmed from the knowledge Lewis might walk out of her life.

"No. There is nothing you can say to justify your omission. All that time, I believed you were here to stay, to continue your uncle's legacy, to… to…" once again, Ailsa ran out of words, so she stomped in circles willing her normally sensible brain to produce an irrefutable case.

Lewis watched her, riveted by the way her hair billowed around her head in a fiery cloud, errant curls bobbing like coiled springs in concert with her erratic steps. Her green eyes glinted with annoyance, but there was also something else — a hint of sorrow, which triggered his next, and totally impetuous reaction.

He grabbed one of Ailsa's flailing wrists, drew her against him, and kissed her… hard.

Ailsa sucked in an incredulous breath. *What the dickens does he think he is doing? Has he no scruples? Where is the gentleman baron I have come to know and lo—* her tumbling questions careened to a juddering halt.

Finally, that which was all but slapping her in the face dawned on Ailsa, and her protest… perfunctory as it was… died on her lips.

"Lewis," she murmured against his mouth several delectable seconds later.

"Yes, my love?"

The endearment rolled over Ailsa like a caress; her heart skipped a beat, and her body tingled. *Was this happening? Was it real? They… well, Lewis… had just flouted every unwritten rule, and it could not be undone. Did she want it to be undone? Absolutely not. What had Lady Travers said? Sometimes one has to reach for the dream. Was this what she meant?* There was only one way to find out.

Fixing Lewis with as severe a look as she could summon up… not easy in the circumstances… she grilled, "Is this the most chivalrous way to answer my questions?"

"I deduced it to be the only means to get a word in edge-ways," his voice laced with humour.

"What if I renewed my inquisition?" a little imp in Ailsa's head prompted her to goad.

"Then I should be left with no alternative."

"Than to…"

"Repeat the manoeuvre." He twinkled down at her.

"You make it sound as though we are on opposing sides of a conflict." She felt his lips graze her nose, then brush her ear, any and all eminently rational dissension melting away like dew under the heat of the sun.

"I think perhaps until this moment we were, but I am convinced the peace negotiations will prove more than satisfactory and an entente can be reached. Now hush while I lay out my terms…"

His persuasive techniques banished any lingering qualms regarding the veracity of his claim.

"Will you?" Ailsa ventured when they came up for air, twiddling absently with one of the buttons on his jacket.

"Will I what?"

"Leave when the year is up?" Ailsa could not prevent a trace of sadness from creeping into her voice, but she had to ask. She had to know.

"I have duties in London, I cannot shirk." Feeling her wriggle in an attempt to disentangle herself from his arms, he tightened his embrace. "Stay there." He kissed her forehead.

"Before you start another fight, compelling us to reestablish our treaty," he waggled his brows, eliciting a low laugh, "my decision to stay, although secured in the last few moments, was already determined. You were correct in your avowal that this place burrows under your skin.

"Truth be told, I was resentful when I learnt about the will. What did I need with an estate so far from the city, it might as well be the moon. Not even the promise of a marquisate was enough to convince me. It was mama who insisted I come. Some tarradiddle about finding myself. My plan was to see out the year and not one day more.

"When I arrived, I could not believe the apparent dilapidation of the house, then I stepped inside. I have never felt so bound to a place so instantly. It was as though I had come home, a sentiment I found hard to divine and, thus, ignored. I struggled to adjust to the quiet, to the melody of birdsong instead of the rattle of carts and carriages, the constant ebb and flow of voices but, before many days had passed, the notion of returning to the cacophony that is London became less attractive.

"Your passion for this land, this ancient and immutable land is contagious, encouraging me to see it through your eyes, gaining a perspective not jaded by circumstance.

"Have I, in mama's quixotic terms, found myself? Perhaps, although I beg you not to tell her. She will gloat. Given I was unaware I was lost, I daresay it is open to debate, but I have discovered a sense of belonging, which could amount to the same thing.

"Returning to your question. I foresee splitting my year between London and Whispering Pines. This place has so much potential; to abandon it would be a travesty." He paused and, sliding a light finger under her chin, tilted her face to hold her wary gaze. "Do you know anyone who might be interested in forming an alliance to achieve that objective?"

Ailsa clamped her lips together to stop them trembling. His answer was more than a clarification; it was a commitment. She stared into his arresting eyes, their hue in the sunshine akin to that of the crystal-clear lakes so distinctive of this region. She saw herself reflected there, along with an emotion so profound her knees all but buckled.

"Ailsa?" She heard his anxiety at her reticence and, although in her heart she knew, she needed an unequivocal declaration.

"I may know of one person, but it is crucial she hears the parameters of the aforementioned alliance before any collaboration can commence."

He smiled that same lazy smile, Ailsa recalled from Christmas Day.

"Ailsa Duval, I love you. I think I have always loved you, but my focus was so far removed from anything remotely associated with courtship, I had not the wit to identify that which ought to have been unmistakeable.

"Might you put a grumpy baron out of his misery and do me the greatest honour of becoming my wife? I promise to devote my life to your happiness, and love you until the lakes run dry."

As declarations went, that was about as unequivocal as it could get.

Chapter Eighteen

A radiant smile lit Ailsa's delicate features. She stretched out her hand, gentle fingers tracing the side of his face from his temple, along his cheek, coming to rest at the corner of his mouth. Lifting up on tiptoe, she pressed her lips to his.

"I love you more than life itself."

Her simple yet heartfelt admission, emulating his own thoughts of the previous evening did more to convince him of her devotion than any flowery speech.

By the time the pair returned to the vicarage, Lady Travers and Gervase, ensconced in the drawing room, sipping coffee, and working their way through a plate of freshly baked biscuits, were engrossed in a discussion about the topic of the upcoming Sunday sermon.

Gervase eyed the couple over his spectacles. "I take it, you have resolved your differences."

Unaccountably shy, Ailsa blushed as Lewis nodded. "We

have, sir and, further to our earlier conversation, might I beg your blessing?"

"You asked her?"

"I did."

"Ailsa?" Gervase looked at his daughter. "Lord Anner-sleigh sought my permission to request your hand in marriage, which I had no hesitation in granting, on the proviso you reciprocate his affection." His genial features creased, and he continued dryly, "Your expression indicates you have no objections to his proposal."

"Not a single one." Ailsa hugged her father. "Arguably, it might seem impulsive, but the foundation of our..." her already pink cheeks flaring with hectic colour. "...errr... affinity was laid weeks, possibly months, ago."

"Of which we are well aware," the vicar observed. "The only people incognisant, were you two."

"It is transparent to me who has been in your company scant days," Lady Travers interjected, "and means your pretence is no longer necessary. Shall your betrothal be announced at the party?"

Lewis and Ailsa exchanged glances. Neither was comfortable being the centre of attention.

"Is that really necessary?" Ailsa rejoined diffidently.

"My dear, everyone in the neighbourhood will rejoice in your happiness and wish to express their goodwill. Would you deny them the chance to celebrate? The evening is already organised, offering the perfect platform." Lewis' mother contested reasonably

Ailsa rolled her eyes. "I agree with your rationale, but we must not forget Lady Delia. To deflect focus from her might result in unwelcome repercussions. Mayhap we ought to wait, and have you announce it, say a week tomorrow in church? It is only a delay of two days," she appealed to her father who dipped his head.

"In truth, a preferable alternative, and makes our betrothal more personal." Lewis reached for and squeezed Ailsa's fingers gently. She smiled at him, loving that they were in agreement.

"Capital notion, capital." Gervase beamed affably.

On that note, Ailsa rang for more refreshments, while Gervase launched into a lively commentary about weddings, which proved an effective and pertinent distraction.

When the visitors took their leave, Lewis felt moved to say, "Are you certain you are content to wait a week? While I concur with your reservations regarding Lady Delia, this is our life together, she ought not have a role in our decision. We could announce it this afternoon. I, for one, would like to shout it from the top of the church right now." He held Ailsa's gaze.

"Absopositively, although I should like to see you proclaiming your intent from the bell tower. That would set tongues wagging." Ailsa replied, calmly contracting the two affirmations without blinking. "Not upsetting Lady Delia aside, I like that it is only known to we four. A delicious secret however ephemeral. You?"

"Positolutely," with an unrepentant smirk, Lewis reversed the contraction, to the amusement of the other three. "Come Mama, back to reality. Luncheon and an afternoon of games, I understand."

He made a show of straightening his shoulders. "Once more into the breach, dear friends, once more," he quoted lugubriously, then tucked his mother's hand around his arm, and the two set off back to the manor, turning to wave before they disappeared out of sight.

. . .

Alisa watched them until they were out of sight, admiring Lewis' upright bearing. *He really was ridiculously handsome, and tall, and...* pulling herself together, she closed the door and turned to lean against the cool wood. Alone in the hall, she basked in the raft of delectable sensations Lewis' proposal... his gallant, romantic, and utterly swoon-worthy proposal... had engendered.

The old grandfather clock counted the seconds in muted ticks — ten, twenty. Before it reached thirty, practicality intervened and Ailsa retreated to the library, resuming the task temporarily suspended by what turned out to be a momentous visit by the baron and his mother.

The subsequent week was the longest and the shortest of Ailsa's life. She wanted to slow down time to luxuriate in her secret. On one hand, the clandestine encounters with Lewis when everyone else was otherwise occupied were utterly intoxicating; on the other, she could not wait for their betrothal to be public knowledge.

In between stolen kisses and murmured endearments, they talked about anything and everything. As though now they had found the courage to confess their innermost feelings, a dam had burst and the emotions flooding out could scarcely be contained.

One important, if serious subject — despite his assurance it was too distressing for ladies' ears — concerned Lewis' time in the recent wars.

"You have witnessed abominations beyond comprehension, which, I imagine, continue to haunt you. Although you try to consign those memories to the farthest recesses of your mind, that is not enough to banish, merely suppress. They will lurk and prowl, festering until, when you least expect it rear up like malevolent ghosts to torment.

"You need to talk about it until it is less... immediate. I need to gain an insight and, hopefully, some understanding of what you experienced. I am not so presumptuous as to claim I can alleviate your nightmares, but knowing the cause might help me to help you overcome them. Do you see?" Ailsa implored.

Lewis, who had steadfastly refused to be drawn on this topic save when he met with fellow veterans of the conflict, could not deny her argument bore weight, yet tried to deflect.

"I accept the premise but..."

"Lewis," she cajoled, employing her most winsome smile, "do you trust me?"

"With my life." He smiled at her earnest expression.

"Then trust me enough to bare your soul. Soon our lives shall be inextricably entwined, but a marriage is not a true union if we cannot be honest with each other."

"Fair enough," he capitulated, and since had unburdened himself little by little... it was not a tale to be told in one sitting... to Ailsa's outward relief and inward consternation. The latter she admitted to her father through whom she gained an objective perspective and a consoling shoulder.

Although the betrothal was not official, the shift in the relationship between the baron and the vicar's daughter was subtle but palpable... if one knew what to look for.

Their perforce minimal, given the house party, interactions revealed an intimacy previously dismissed as fanciful and now embraced. While they did not flaunt their new-found happiness, neither did they see any reason to conceal it.

"A leap of faith it might be but, by acquainting everyone, and by everyone, I mean Lady Delia with our courtship in so gradual a fashion, we hope to avert any… reckless conduct," Ailsa had said diplomatically when explaining their reasoning to her father and Lewis' mother.

"One can only pray," Lady Travers had replied tartly, with a distinct lack of certitude.

Ever the optimist, Gervase had contended, "I am sure common sense will come to the fore."

Lewis did not voice his opinion, but his glance at Ailsa informed her of his scepticism. If ever there was a contradiction in terms it was that Lady Delia possessed common sense.

Listening to the chatter wafting around him, something pulled at his mind. A scene the previous week when Lady Delia had encountered Odin on the staircase. The former had growled and batted at the young lady who, discretion being the better part of valour, had taken a judiciously wide berth, muttering dire threats at the grey monster.

Lewis had long recognised animals were better judges of character than the majority of humans, and Odin's antipathy towards that young lady spoke volumes.

He would trust the cat before he trusted Lady Delia.

Most, despite the length of time it had taken the two in question to acknowledge their affection, viewed the transition as felicitous and a natural progression — wisely avoiding *any* mention of how many wagers had been laid amongst themselves as to when not if.

One hardly noticed, and one was furious.

Lady Delia, not about to have her plans upskittled by a trumped-up nobody, brooded over the problem at length. One evening at dinner, three days before the party, the glimmer of an idea began to brew on the edge of her consciousness.

She let it percolate.

It had merit and was relatively simple to accomplish. Timing was crucial.

Yes, the more she ruminated over it, the more favourable it became.

Chapter Nineteen

Marianne was troubled. Delia's temperament, never particularly sedate, verged on the volatile. One minute she was petulant, the next almost manic in her glee. Surmising it related to the baron, and Delia's determination to 'win him', Marianne vacillated over whether to alert someone about her misgivings.

Muffled up against the chilly air, she trudged around the gardens, mulling over a range of approaches, only to discount each one as ludicrous. That she needed to warn *anyone* about the possibility of a maybe, sounded melo-dramatic.

Who to tell was another conundrum. After discounting Lord Annersleigh because he was the object of Delia's interest and their host to boot, the logical choice was Lady Travers. Marianne remained reluctant, unwilling to solicit advice from the countess who had so generously extended the invitation to join her at Whispering Pines.

Meandering along the neat paths delineating dormant flower beds, she toyed with the notion of confiding in Ailsa. Although they had met only a handful of times, Marianne had gained the impression the vicar's daughter was an astute young lady and, her presumed courtship with the baron aside, would offer sound and practical guidance without making one feel as though one was meddling unnecessarily.

Unfortunately, once Delia got a scheme in her head, she became like a dog with a bone, and anyone who tried to interfere was likely to get bitten.

Deep in thought, her head down, Marianne did not hear the crunch of boots on the gravel, nor a gaily spoken greeting. Frustrated with her lack of answers, she huffed a weighty sigh.

"Goodness, you nearly blew me over," a cheerful voice exclaimed.

Startled, Marianne raised her head to see the focus of her musings studying her with friendly curiosity. "Oh, Miss Duval, forgive me, I was… err… wool-gathering."

Adept at reading expressions, Ailsa caught the unease Marianne had tried to mask, along with her, almost imperceptible, hesitation. "Is something amiss, Miss Fletcher?" she asked kindly. "You seem distrait."

Marianne swithered. She started to speak several times then clamped her lips together, torn between imparting her suspicions and betraying her friend.

"My dear, nothing ought to be so worrisome, you cannot unburden yourself." With typical insouciance, Ailsa hooked her arm through Marianne's, urging her beyond the formal gardens and, skirting the lawns, struck out towards the Great Park.

There was no one else abroad, the tranquility broken only by the cawing of a rook or distant chuff of a deer.

Gossamer-like, a mist lingered above the quiescent earth, stubbornly refusing to disperse despite a trenchant campaign by the weak winter sun whose hazy beams threaded through the leafless trees to create labyrinthine patterns across the ground. Here and there in secluded corners, hints of new growth — the promise of spring.

The air was cool yet fresh, heady almost and, carried on the gentle breeze, a delicate fragrance, which Marianne had come to associate with this isolated estate. One she would miss when she left.

By way of distraction, Ailsa launched into a monologue of mundanities, which did not require a response from Marianne, leaving her to ponder.

When they reached the lake, nestled on the boundary between the neatly manicured lawns and the untamed parkland, Marianne had arrived at a decision.

"I have a dilemma."

"That I deduced," Ailsa teased smilingly. "I imagine it has something to do with Lady Delia."

Marianne's jaw dropped and she gaped at Ailsa in a most unladylike fashion. "How… when… did you… except…" collecting herself, she tried again. "How on earth did you guess?"

"'Tis not very complicated. You are Lady Delia's friend. I expect she has alluded to something with which you are not comfortable and hope to avert before it results in a spot of theatrics causing her, and by extension you, indignity. Am I close?"

Marianne stunned by Ailsa's intuition, could only nod in a speechless daze.

"Come, let us sit on this bench and have a tête-à-tête. Just because I do not live in London, does not mean I am unfamiliar with the ambitions of those who do."

"Perhaps I ought not embroil you in this, it may be nothing…" Marianne started dubiously.

Ailsa said gently, "If it is, all well and good and no harm done. Miss Fletcher —"

"Oh, do please drop the Miss Fletcher. Marianne will

suffice. Sometimes honorifics get in the way, do you not agree?" Marianne beseeched.

"I concur… and on the proviso you call me Ailsa. Miss Duval makes me sound like a maiden aunt." Ailsa mimed an old crone wagging her finger, making Marianne giggle, and the hint of tension eased. "Now, before you talk yourself out of it a second time, consider me more discreet than a priest in a confessional. I guarantee you will feel better once it is out in the open… as it were."

Leaning against the back of the bench, Ailsa stretched out her legs — to all the world as though she was doing nothing more than admiring the ever-changing reflections in the translucent surface of the lake.

"I think it might help if I provide a little background," Marianne began shyly, choosing her words carefully so as not to break a confidence, becoming less guarded as she warmed to her recitation.

"Delia had her heart broken. At least, that is what she persists in declaring to anyone prepared to listen. In truth, I believe her pride took the beating not her heart."

Marianne explained about the severed courtship. "Lord Baudwin plied his suit assiduously and appeared besotted with Delia who expected him to propose, as did the rest of the *ton*. I do not like the man, he is too…" she racked her brain for the best description, plumping for… "…suave." Her nose crinkled in distaste, as an image of the bounder swam across her vision.

"Too suave? Ahhh, as in obsequious? A trifle unctuous?" Ailsa guessed.

"Precisely. He made my skin crawl, and I never felt entirely… clean when I had been in his company." Marianne could not quite suppress a shudder. "Had he treated her like a gentleman should, we would not be having this conversation, but he is the worst kind of rake. Gaming hells and brothels are his entertainment of choice and, it came to light, the only reason he was courting Delia was because her dowry would clear his debts."

Twisting to face Ailsa, Marianne's eyes were anguished. "Who does that? Deliberately turn on the charm until someone is hanging onto your every word, believes your devotion is real, that you are a knight in shining armour. Delia has her faults, none of us is perfect, but she does not deserve to be treated dishonourably."

"An utter scoundrel," Ailsa said flatly. "Poor Delia." Pity for the young lady's predicament mitigating her exasperation over Delia's professed — to Marianne and overheard by Lewis — intentions.

"Regrettably, her reaction was less... reserved than is approved and, for a while, she was not shunned exactly but there was a definite cold shoulder from some of her peers. Lady Travers' invitation was providential. Now this..." Marianne stopped.

"Now what?" Ailsa pressed. "The crux of your confusion must be enunciated for it to lose its power," she coaxed.

Blowing an even more forceful sigh, Marianne repeated the conversation of which Ailsa was already aware, adding her apprehension about Delia's fickle demeanour. "I fear her desire to exact a little revenge on Lord Baudwin exceeds her ability to think rationally. In her mind, returning to London on the arm of a man about to inherit a marquisate will not only stifle the gossips but is also a very public way of thumbing her nose at her erstwhile suitor," Marianne concluded miserably.

Ailsa sought to placate, "While your concern for Lady Delia is commendable, you cannot legislate for her actions. They are not yours to shoulder. Do not fret," when Marianne opened her mouth in rebuttal, "let us try to outwit her.

Observation is key. We must ensure she cannot achieve her goal."

Reading Marianne's irresolute expression correctly, Ailsa instilled a stringent note into her voice. "In the same vein that Lady Delia did not deserve to be treated shabbily, Lord Annersleigh does not deserve to have his hospitality or his reputation compromised by a wilful madam who cares for no one but herself."

"Ailsa…"

"Marianne, loyalty to your friend is one thing… and I applaud you for it, but you must see that Delia is behaving like a spoilt child. I understand, she suffered an ignominy, but rather than rise above it, she is allowing it to fester, to the point she hopes to trick an innocent man into a liaison he does not want. This is not all about her. Several lives will be ruined if she succeeds."

Ailsa realised she had hit a nerve when Marianne straightened her spine, literally and figuratively.

"What shall we do."

Chapter Twenty

Despite a mixed week weather-wise, Friday dawned bright and sunny. Blue sky, a smattering of fluffy white clouds, and a blustery breeze dried the damp roads and tracks leading to the manor.

Whispering Pines bustled with final preparations. Several guests, required to travel a reasonable distance, had been invited to stay overnight. Rooms were readied and fires lit to banish any lingering chill from being closed up for an extended period.

Bouquets of flowers and bowls of fruit graced sideboards, cabinets, and tables, mirrored in the polished surfaces. Boughs of laurel and pine with their uplifting scent adorned the mantels, while trailing greenery was intertwined around the balustrade of the sweeping staircase.

Ailsa contended that not even the Regent himself would be able to find fault with the decorations. "Had he been invited and felt disposed to attend," she qualified glibly.

His desire to hide in the library with Odin for the duration undiminished, Lewis was, nevertheless, effusive in his praise for Mrs Staples and her staff for their sterling efforts.

"You have done yourselves proud." He smiled his appreciation, and proposed, once the guests had departed, an extra day off for everyone, which was received with barely suppressed jubilation.

By mid-afternoon, coach after coach rattled up the driveway, disgorging their exquisitely attired passengers who, after being asked whether they would like to freshen up, were either escorted to their bedchambers or ushered into the stately drawing room where drinks and savouries would be served.

Before long, the clink of glass and china mingled with the light-hearted chatter of new arrivals as introductions were made, people drifted, conversations swirled, and the fleeting camaraderie induced by social occasions began.

Ailsa had suggested the food be served buffet-style, rather than a formal sit-down meal, so as not to disrupt the smooth flow of the evening. This had a two-fold benefit in that not only did it minimise the pressure on the kitchen staff to produce numerous dishes all at once but also negated the obligation to find extra banqueting tables in order to seat such a large assemblage.

Strains of music filtered from the impromptu ballroom… otherwise known as the Great Hall… where a local quintet played an astonishingly varied repertoire, including the current most popular pieces, tempting their listeners to take to the floor.

With a mind to all possibilities simmering in the background, Lewis asked his mother to partner him for the first dance, which galvanised other couples to join them and soon, the room was alive with colour and movement.

As the evening wore on Lewis, at his most urbane, danced with Lady Delia and then Miss Fletcher, before introducing them to one or two of the local bachelors who were gratifyingly attentive.

Marianne, especially, found herself questioning how important titles actually were because Mr Liam Davidson with his sparkling blue eyes, unruly dark hair, and toe-curling smile, made her wish she had the courage to throw caution to the wind and elope to Gretna Green in a heartbeat.

Right at this moment, she did not care whether he was a farmer or a prince, thrilled that he seemed equally entranced by her. To the amusement of their peers, who were polite enough not to remark upon it, the pair spent the entire evening together, oblivious to anything else going on around them.

Lady Delia on the other hand, while accepting several requests to dance was not interested in a dalliance with any of the young bucks, however handsome… her lip curling in a discontented sneer at the very notion. Her eye was well and truly fixed on Lord Annersleigh, who was dancing his *fourth* set with that baggage from the vicarage.

Ignoring the fact, this was a tacit declaration of intent on Lewis' part, Delia reviewed her plan, which she deemed brilliant and infallible, unaware she had not checked the cunning smile which played about her lips as she envisioned the outcome.

By dawn tomorrow, she would be betrothed to her host and, by summer's end, a marchioness.

Catching Delia's expression, while being twirled around the dance floor to a Mozart waltz, Ailsa knew the young lady's scheme was on the cusp of unfolding.

"We must be on our guard," she murmured to Lewis as the quintet finished on a flourish. "Whatever crackpot scheme Delia has concocted will be put in motion tonight, of that I am convinced. She cannot risk delaying."

"Do you have an inkling of her plan?"

"No, but I surmise as long as you stay close to me, your mama, or one of your friends, you are safe. Do not, and I cannot emphasise this strongly enough, go anywhere on your own."

"The devil, beg pardon, but surely you cannot suspect…"

"That is exactly what I suspect. She wants a husband, she wants a title, and you are, in her mind, ripe for the plucking."

Unable to help himself, Lewis shot her a lascivious grin. "There is only one lady to whom I will grant permission to indulge in any kind of plucking." He leant back in anticipation of her response.

On cue, she jabbed his brocade waistcoat. "Lord Annersleigh, for shame, you are a rogue."

"Yes, but I am your rogue, for evaaaah…" he taunted wickedly, drawing out the last word and flexing his fingers in a mock sinister curl.

"Oh you…" she spluttered with laughter and batted him on the chest to no discernible effect. Chuckling, Lewis looped her hand around his arm, and the couple headed to the dining room eager to partake of the sumptuous delicacies on offer, unaware their every step was monitored.

Sitting on the edge of her bed twiddling the filmy silk of her, specifically chosen, nightgown between her fingers absently, Delia watched the clock on the mantel, questioning whether the minute hand was frozen, so gradually did it move.

Midnight was a forgotten hour, and the guests had either gone home or sought their beds. She had loitered in the drawing room sipping a cup of tea to ensure she was one of the last to come upstairs.

Quietly, she opened her door and peered out. The corridor was in darkness. The gloom alleviated only by the pale moonbeams filtering through the huge stained-glass window, and a couple of candelabra — which shed sufficient light that an individual could wander the halls without tripping.

Cocking her head, Delia listened intently. The household seemed to be asleep. Still, she waited — it would not do to be precipitous.

Another half an hour ticked by with ever decreasing slowness. Finally, she deemed it safe to implement her plan.

Shrugging into a diaphanous dressing gown, Delia crept along the hall, glad of the thick runner under her bare feet, muffling her steps. Unerringly, she crossed the gallery, following the curve of the banister to Lord Annersleigh's quarters. Silent as a mouse, she turned the handle of the heavy oak door, relieved when it swung open without so much as a creak.

Tiptoeing inside, Delia surveyed the baron's private domain, admiring the decor which, although unequivocally masculine was not austere. The pleasant warmth drew her gaze to the flames leaping in the grate, and she was momentarily mesmerised by the way they writhed and cavorted around the massive hunks of wood, sparks exploding in soft 'poofs' to disappear up the chimney.

Carefully, she pivoted on her heel and squinted at the bed, spying a bulge under the covers.

Perfect.

Chapter Twenty-One

The great fourposter, its rich blue brocade hangings to protect its occupant from any draught was cast into deep shadow, obscuring details.

A slight dip in the pillow, and a suspicion of hair around which the covers were tucked, persuaded Delia the baron was fast asleep.

Soundlessly, she padded to the side of the bed opposite to where the hump lay, instinctively stroking the crisp white linens, and twitching the luxurious eiderdown delicately, in approval.

The awkward-shaped lump seemed to stretch. Delia held her breath and squinted, relieved when it appeared she had not disturbed her quarry.

The outline *did* looked rather odd, stunted almost, but she presumed it was trick of the firelight flickering in the darkness.

It was now or never.

Mustering up her courage, Delia discarded her dressing gown, and eased between the sheets.

She stretched out one hand.

Instead of soft cotton or... better yet... skin, her fingers sank into thick, velvety fluffiness.

Taken by surprise, Odin shot out from under the covers, hissing his outrage, fur sticking out like a teasel and twice as bristly, landing on Delia's head, his claws snarling into her elaborately coiffured blonde hair.

Forgetting her mission and blinded by the cat's body draped across her face, Delia screamed in panic. Gyrating frantically, she made a desperate attempt to dislodge whatever horror had ensnared her, which encouraged Odin to tighten his grip.

Delia's shrieks woke Lady Travers whose suite was adjacent to her son's. Questioning whether the manor was under attack by vagabonds, the countess leapt out of bed, pulled on her dressing gown, and burst into the corridor. Quite what she expected to do if faced with marauding bandits was anyone's guess — something, much *much* later, her son felt moved to remark upon.

Pausing momentarily, Lady Travers registered that the pained bellows came from Lewis' rooms. Reaching the door, she came to a stunned standstill. In the middle of the bedchamber, a dishevelled Delia sporting the, undoubtedly, latest fashion in millinery... a huge grey cat... pirouetted in wild abandon, squealing, "Murder mittens," an insult which had absolutely no effect on Odin.

Despite the gravity of the circumstance, and thankful the overnight guests were in the east wing, out of earshot, Lady Travers was hard pushed to keep a straight face. The scene was funnier than a pantomime. Stifling her laughter, she approached the duo — Odin refusing to release his victim and Delia pleading for help — to try to extricate the cat.

"Be still, Delia," she ordered. "I cannot do anything until you stop jiggling about."

"Get this overgrown rat off my head," Delia begged piteously, certain she was about to lose half of her hair.

"Then stand still," Lady Travers snapped in a tone which brooked no argument.

The fight went out of Delia who wilted, but did not stop wailing as, painstakingly, Lady Travers unhooked Odin's claws.

Eventually cat and hair were untangled, strands of the latter strewn on the bedcovers. Odin, alternately spitting and growling, his hackles in a stiff ridge along his back, strutted over to the fire, curled up on the stool near the hearth and glowered at his adversary.

Her head smarting, Delia sobbed, but her relief was short-lived.

"Explain yourself, young lady."

Delia struggled to face her interrogator. "Lord Anner-sleigh wanted me to join him. He invited me here. He wants to m…" she faltered under Lady Travers' steely glare.

"Do not even think about justifying your actions with falsehoods," the countess barked. "How dare you try to inveigle my son, to trick him into a union he does not want? Have you, for a single moment, considered how many lives you were about to ruin had Odin not thwarted your plan?" Incensed was an understatement — a tempest would seem tranquil by comparison.

"Not only have you abused my son's hospitality, but also you have breached my trust, and disrespected this house. You cared not one fig for the distress your behaviour would cause Miss Duval and her family.

"Never mind the damage you might have wrought here, what of your poor parents? What if rumour of this reaches Society? I am sure your mama hopes you make a good match, but not at the expense of others. You are not a child, Delia, you are approaching your majority. Perhaps it is time you started acting your age.

"The whole purpose of my invitation was to give you some separation from the sorrow Lord Baudwin caused. A time to heal, to take stock and reevaluate your life. Not to fabricate a more egregious scandal.

"At least 'twas only you and he affected by the initial upset. Had this charade been successful, the ramifications would be unthinkable. To say I am ashamed and appalled would be to trivialise the strength of my emotions."

Striving for control, Lady Travers took a steadying breath. "You are fortunate it was I who rescued you from Odin. I suggest you return to your bed and take a long hard look at yourself. You have left me no alternative but to leave the manor on the morrow. We may only get as far as the first coaching inn, but better there than here where you cannot be trusted to behave like the daughter of an earl you are."

Cursorily, Lady Travers smoothed the bedclothes, brushing wisps of hair onto the floor, grabbed the discarded dressing gown, then all but shoved Delia out of the room and along the hall. If anyone else was disturbed by the racket, they had decided not to interfere, and the house was quiet.

Unable to stay her tongue, Delia heard herself implore wretchedly, "I do not understand, where is Lord Annersleigh?"

"I can hazard a guess, but that is not your business. Bed for you." The countess opened Delia's door and waited for the girl to enter. "Do not try my patience by scurrying back to the baron's rooms. I am about to request a footman to keep watch. Go on."

Satisfied she had put the fear of God into Delia, Lady Travers rang for Craddock, who listened to her instructions sleepily at first, then with sharp focus.

"You can rely on me, my lady," he assured and, finding a chair, remained a silent sentinel for the reminder of the night, not moving even when Lewis returned in the wee small hours unaware of what had transpired in his absence.

Had Delia taken time to observe her surroundings instead of focusing on her own plot, she might have noticed her host left the house at the end of the party.

While farewelling his guests, Lewis fell into a discussion with Lambert Duval who, along with his family, was staying with his father overnight, and somehow ended up walking to the vicarage where he was pressed into a brandy and a hot chocolate, much to his betrothed's delight.

Relaxing in the cosy ambience of the vicarage library, conversation flowed, a second brandy poured, and another hot drink brewed. The hours flew by, and it was only when the clock on the mantel chimed four did any of them register dawn was closer than midnight.

"Gracious, we have talked the night away," Lewis exclaimed contritely. "How unconscionably rude of me."

"Fret not." Gervase waved a hand in gentle dismissal of Lewis' apology. "Many's the time Ailsa and I sit up 'til sunrise putting the world to rights. Nice you feel comfortable enough to join us without time registering."

Lewis grinned an acknowledgement and took his leave, Lambert and he vowing to keep in touch now they had reconnected. "Sometimes the only people who understand are those with shared experience," Lambert said as the two men shook hands.

Agreeing, Lewis could not help but glance at Ailsa whose,

"I told you so," rang in his ears a second time. She met his gaze guilelessly.

"I shall see Lewis out," Ailsa offered, hoping to sneak in a goodnight kiss. Her father nodded as Mr Phelps appeared to ask whether Lewis might like to borrow a cloak.

"'Tis a bitter night, my lord," the genial retainer worried.

"Thank you, Mr Phelps, I should be glad of one." Lewis accepted with a smile. "At least it is not snowing."

Ailsa, a green woollen wrap slung around her shoulders, walked Lewis to the door.

"I shall see you on the morrow." He bowed over her hand, turning it to kiss her palm.

"'Tis already the morrow." Ailsa shivered in the chill night air, prompting Lewis — undeterred by the fact it was inappropriate, and her family were mere feet away — to tuck her against him.

"Mayhap, but a few hours of darkness remain. Get you inside, where 'tis warm." He brushed his lips to her nose, rewarded with a soft sigh. His arms tightened around her, and he revelled in the sensation of her body moulded to his.

"Do not get waylaid by ne'er do wells," Ailsa murmured, lifting up on tiptoe to return his kiss soundly.

Lewis spluttered with mirth. "Here, in the back of beyond? This is not one of your adventure stories."

"Not all mischief makers are found on the road." She smiled, squeezed his hand, and hurried into the vicarage, leaving Lewis scratching his head at her cryptic comment.

Which came back to him when he came across a watchful Craddock sitting outside his bedchamber.

"Is something amiss, Craddock?" he asked in undertones.

"A minor disturbance," Craddock replied placidly. "Lady Travers dealt with it but requested my presence to ensure it was not repeated."

"You must be exhausted. Go, find your bed."

"Don't you worry, Lord Annersleigh."

Clearly, Craddock had no intention of moving. Apparently, his mother's word carried more weight... *so much for being lord of the manor*, Lewis thought wryly. "Fine, but I do not want to see you on duty until Sunday." Keenly aware that too would fall on deaf ears, but he had at least tried.

"My lord." Craddock dipped his head.

Lewis bade him goodnight... what little of it there was left... and entered his quarters.

He frowned at the state of his bedclothes, which looked to have been disturbed then remade in a hurry. Too tired to fathom the reason, he completed his nightly routine, and slid between the sheets, falling asleep in seconds.

Chapter Twenty-Two

The various activities of the previous night saw the household emerge in dribs and drabs.

Lewis, in spite of the brevity of his slumber woke, as was his habit, with the dawn, rolling over to find Odin alongside him, rumbling like a distant thunderstorm.

He buried his fingers into the feline's warm fur, prompting a stretch, the flaunting of a very fluffy belly expecting to be tickled, accompanied by a deeper purr… if that was possible. The epitome of contentment, Odin shuffled closer, nudging his great head under Lewis' chin.

"You are demanding this morning." Lewis stroked the creature. "Did you perchance have your own party on my bed last night? Does that explain the rumpled sheets?"

Odin declined to affirm or deny the accusation, fixing Lewis with a hard stare as though galled by the frivolous notion he would deign to entertain.

Lewis chuckled. "Forgive me, your highness. I stand corrected. Something happened while I was out, and I mean to get to the bottom of it."

Much as it would be nice to lie abed, he was wide awake and, with marked reluctance, got up.

He ate breakfast in isolated splendour, relishing the peace and quiet before the hordes descended.

Lady Travers was next to appear, Miss Fletcher on her heels, neither of whom mentioned anything untoward happening the previous night in their subdued, not quite awake, chatter.

His mother met his quirked eyebrow with an artless smile. Never a good sign, and Lewis ruminated over whether Ailsa's caution had come to fruition. *Surely not.*

Quite clever with puzzles, he combed through his brain, collecting seemingly random pieces of information, and slotting them together. The picture they formed elicited a groan he forgot to suppress. Suddenly, the room felt very cold despite the fire blazing in the hearth.

Never had he been so thankful for an impromptu conversation.

"A word when I've eaten," quietly, Lady Travers interrupted his train of thought.

Lewis nodded distractedly. "Of course, of course. I must—"

"Not until we have spoken," she cut him off.

Overhearing their exchange, Marianne was bewildered, then she recalled being disturbed in the early hours. *Had Delia...?* Assuredly, she had.

Mentally and with frustration, Marianne palmed her forehead. *Of all the addlepated, bird witted, irresponsible, nincompoops, Delia Groves takes the cake, and the biscuits, and the pies. How the dickens was she going to talk her way out of this?*

Marianne closed her eyes, unable to equate the friend she,

until this morning, thought she knew with the person who had apparently thought it appropriate to hoodwink a baron.

"I am sorry," she blurted out.

Two faces stared at her in astonishment.

"What on earth for?" Lewis asked.

"This is about Delia is it not?" She did not wait for an answer. "I knew she might try something. I sincerely hope she has not brought shame on her family."

"Thankfully, not, although I do believe we ought to depart the manor today, even if we only reach the closest coaching inn," Lady Travers replied, reiterating what she had said to Delia.

"Mama, no. There is no call to leave so abruptly," Lewis refuted. "I am certain Lady Delia will not attempt a repeat of whatever happened last night. A word, nay a single look, from you is enough to make grown men weep. A young lady is no match for your ire."

"You make me sound like an ogre." Lady Travers quipped good-naturedly, and the vaguely strained atmosphere lightened.

"Just a protective mother." Lewis grinned, "but I mean it. 'Tis only two more days," he wheedled. "It is a shame to cut your visit short and rush away over a silly chit losing her common sense."

Lady Travers vacillated, unaware Marianne was holding her breath, her secret… her delicious secret… hanging in the balance.

Yielding to her son's logic, grateful an afternoon of frantic packing… at least, the supervision thereof… was not in her immediate future, Lady Travers capitulated, and Marianne gave a soundless exhale of relief.

"Given Miss Fletcher seems to be cognisant of her friend's ploy, I see no reason to exclude her from our discussion. What say you, Mama?"

Lady Travers inclined her head. "Fair enough, with the proviso you treat what I have to say with the utmost discretion. Regardless of what transpired, the least said the soonest mended."

She waited until the other two nodded their agreement, then provided an abridged version of Delia's escapade.

The latter's brazen exploits notwithstanding, neither Lewis nor Marianne could restrain their hilarity which reverberated around the dining room. Lady Travers, whose vivid account was worthy of a Covent Garden farce, felt her composure crumbling and shared in their laughter.

Lewis sobered, "Is there any benefit in me confronting Lady Delia? To my mind, compounding her embarrassment is unkind and unnecessary. Perhaps it will be forgotten more quickly if I do not refer to it at all, as though no one considered it important enough to enlighten me.

"For her conduct to have consequences, it needs to be addressed. I have heard it said that a lack of reaction to a circumstance, good or bad, can be worse than acknowledging it. To respond implies I am affected, that she has unsettled me, found a chink in my armour as it were. To ignore it conveys indifference."

"For your part, I agree wholeheartedly. For my part, an interview is essential. This attitude requires nipping in the bud, or the poor child will waste her life seeking the impossible," his mother replied.

"Unless a cast iron arrangement is in place which, in Delia's case is not, status should never take precedence over happiness, and I know all Delia's mother wants is her daughter's happiness, evidenced by her acceptance of that dratted viscount. A lucky escape and no mistake."

"How very modern of you, Mama," Lewis teased.

"I consider myself quite progressive," she rejoined, without rancour.

Breakfast eaten, the two ladies excused themselves claiming sundry tasks. Lewis remained seated, greeting his other guests while his mind churned over his mother's revelation.

He would never understand women, not even the one with whom he had fallen irrevocably in love.

Whatever passed between Lady Travers and Delia was never disclosed, but it was a pensive young lady who joined the others at luncheon. Most attributed her pale face and shadowed eyes to being over-tired or perhaps a trifle discomposed, polite enough not to ply her with questions.

Soft-hearted Marianne urged her friend to join her for a constitutional. "It is much too beautiful an afternoon to languish indoors, especially as in two days we have a long journey during which stretching our legs will be a boon."

Delia smiled her gratitude at Marianne's overture. Excusing themselves from the table, the pair hurried upstairs to don warm cloaks, for the breeze was cool in spite of the bright sunshine and, minutes later, were strolling across the lawns.

Marianne made a valiant bid to spark a conversation, but Delia remained withdrawn as their aimless meandering led them to the lake. The same lake where the former had confessed her troubles to Ailsa. Today, the water was ruffled by eddies of air, reflections forming in the lull only to splinter when gentle zephyrs skimmed the surface.

A bevy of swans floated at the far side, their melodic honk harmonising with the soft quacking of the ducks as they called to one another, and the twitter of birds chasing down unsuspecting insects. The avian refrain and the idyllic scene fostering the perfect composition.

Marianne had to quash an urge to rush back to the manor for her painting materials. To capture this panorama would be a wonderful memory of her holiday, but Delia's need of her took precedence over etchings. She sank onto the bench next to her friend.

"Come, Delia," she coaxed. "A problem shared is a problem halved, and I posit you shall feel lighter of heart once you have entrusted me with the cause of your dejection."

Delia did not reply, her gaze fixed on the ever-changing hues of the lake.

Marianne did not press, merely sat quietly, and waited.

The silence between them was brief.

"I am astonished you care to be seen with me," Delia began diffidently. "My behaviour last night was reprehensible. I allowed ambition to countermand sanity." She flinched in recollection and, involuntarily, her hand touched her sore head. "To be beset by so single-minded an obsession suggests I am deranged, suffering from some kind of mania."

"I did warn you, to be careful," Marianne reminded, but her tone was solicitous. "I think you had better tell me all."

"I suppose…" Delia gave a resigned huff and, haltingly at first, related the night's interlude. No less risible than Lady Travers' version of events, Marianne struggled to contain her mirth — the tale, while pitiful was nonetheless priceless.

Delia's woebegone expression when she concluded was too much and Marianne's unbridled jocularity shattered the afternoon's hush.

"Forgive me, Delia, I sympathise with your plight, but that is the funniest account I have ever heard. "Murder mittens…" she held her sides and tried to regain control. "Oh, oh, I am sorry, but I cannot stop. That deserves honourable mention in the chronicles of Whispering Pines."

"Your consolation warms my heart," Delia groused sarcastically, while unable to prevent her lips twitching. From an objective perspective, Marianne was not erroneous in her conjecture. Then her insecurities reared their heads, and she blew a melancholy sigh. "I have botched things up royally." She blinked back a solitary tear, hating herself for the show of weakness.

Marianne squeezed Delia's arm. "My opinion, for what it is worth, is to view this as a lapse in perspicacity elicited by that wretched viscount. Had he not treated you so callously, we would not be having this conversation. The past cannot be altered but, with the wisdom of hindsight, we can prevent a repeat."

Delia mulled over her friend's words, buoyed by her optimism which was balm to her bruised ego. "Thank you, Marianne, I do not deserve such kindness."

"Oh, pooh," Marianne retorted bracingly. "True friendship ought to be strong enough to survive the odd hiccup…"

"Hiccup? This was more like a drunken sailor's whisky-induced belch," Delia interposed dryly, meeting Marianne's eyes for the first time since they had sat down.

Marianne fought to stem the gurgle threatening to erupt at the image Delia's description conjured up.

It was no use, and the pair burst into giggles, their laughter restoring a friendship, Delia feared she had fractured beyond repair.

Chapter Twenty-Three

Returning to the manor, the drum of hooves caught their attention. A lone rider rattled into the courtyard, at the same moment as Lewis and Ailsa appeared around the corner. Arm in arm, the couple looked a trifle mussed but, thankfully, no one commented.

"Liam," Ailsa exclaimed, surprised to see the young man whose family farm was at the far side of Chesmere. Friends since childhood, neither stood on ceremony with each other. "What brings you here this fine afternoon?"

Mr Davidson dismounted, removed his hat, and bowed. "I hoped, that is, I wondered whether Miss Fletcher might grant me a few moments of her time?" The look he sent Marianne nothing short of smouldering and Marianne's responding smile was luminous.

Astonished, the other three stared, trying to mask their collective confusion.

"Marianne?" Delia, finding her voice, quizzed.

"I made the… errr… acquaintance of Mr Davidson last evening, and he… hmmm… mentioned he might pay a call before we left," Marianne stammered, cheeks aflame.

Ailsa dithered. Under normal circumstances, Marianne ought to have a chaperone. Notwithstanding this, she had proven herself eminently trustworthy and, in relation to the Delia debacle, had demonstrated a sufficiency of virtue without being a prig. Never mind that expecting Marianne to abide by a convention she eschewed was akin to the pot calling the kettle black.

Delia startled everyone by coming to the rescue. "Perhaps my presence at a discreet distance, of course, might offer a solution? I hear the lake makes for an agreeable stroll." She looked at Marianne who beamed her pleasure at this compromise.

"Does that satisfy propriety?" she asked Ailsa who chuckled at the expectant faces awaiting her approval.

"It does," she intoned benevolently.

Observing the interaction with interest, Lewis inter- jected, "Would you like to stay for dinner, Mr Davidson? We are already several, one extra is no hardship."

"Thank you, my lord, that is most kind. I look forward to it." The young man smiled a little shyly.

"Away with you, youngsters." Ailsa flapped them off like an impatient grandmother, ignoring the fact she was scarcely a year their senior.

When Mr Davidson offered Marianne his arm and the pair headed out of the courtyard, Delia hung back.

Looking Lewis square in the eye, she sank a curtsy. "Please accept my sincerest apologies for my abhorrent actions of last night," she began. "No…" when Lewis made to interrupt. "Although your mama says it ill-becomes me to address the subject, I owe you an explanation. My conduct, contrary to your gracious hospitality, was indefensible. I could give you a litany of excuses, none of which are remotely adequate or a justification. I was so caught up in my own… fantasy… I was blind to the damage I could have done."

A hectic wave of colour alleviated her pallor as she swung her gaze between Lewis and Ailsa. "I can only reiterate my regret and pray, one day, you find it in your hearts to forgive me." She turned to follow Marianne.

"Delia." Ailsa, uncaring she had dispensed with titles, halted her exit. "Thank you, that took a great deal of courage. In truth, I knew a little of your aspirations pertaining to the baron. Marianne was worried for you," she elaborated at Delia's obvious bafflement.

"All things considered, although my absence last night was unplanned, it was fortuitous and, in some respects, I ought to thank you for your dastardly scheme." Lewis' lips quirked.

This unlikely disclosure made Delia frown in incomprehension.

Ailsa gave an irreverent snort.

"Had I not overheard you and Miss Fletcher talking, I would not have asked for Ailsa's help, which turned out to be… serendipitous," Lewis said, sharing so sweet a smile with his betrothed, Delia was swamped with relief that a cat, however fiendish, had thwarted her attempt to ruin their happiness.

"Neither of us wishes anything but the best for you. We hope you take only happy memories of your visit here and consign the less agreeable ones to the bonfire where they belong." Ailsa twinkled at the younger woman.

Delia inclined her head. "Your generosity of spirit warms my heart," she murmured. "Few would be so… considerate."

"Oh pooh," unconsciously, Ailsa parroted Marianne. "Yes, it was a nonsensical thing to do. Will you do it again? I doubt it, and I do believe Odin's intervention was… err… timely." Ailsa's grin was nothing short of wicked.

Delia's cheeks went from pink to puce. "He certainly holds the best interests of Lord Annersleigh in his paws," her tone droll.

"I cannot argue there." Lewis smiled. "Now, be off with you. Enjoy the last few days of your visit and do not think on this anymore."

"I shall do my utmost." Delia's solemn features morphed into a wholly unrestrained grin — possibly her first spontaneous gesture since arriving at Whispering Pines — dipped a curtsy, then turned to follow Marianne and Liam, calling, "Wait for me, you two."

"I think she will be fine," Ailsa mused contemplatively, watching the young lady hitch her skirts and dash after her friend.

"I concur," Lewis agreed, then spun Ailsa to face him. "Where were we?"

"Hmm… I cannot recall… remind me." Ailsa's smile was part guileless, part provocative.

"Minx," he chided without heat. "Let me see… here?" he kissed her forehead, "or here?" he grazed his nose down hers then kissed the tip. "Perhaps here." His lips skimmed the sensitive skin behind her ear sending ripples of delight down her spine and turning her knees to water. *Heavens but the man was masterful.*

"No, wait, I am confident it was here…." Glancing around, somewhat belatedly, to ensure they were not observed, Lewis drew Ailsa into a tender embrace and stole her breath in a heart-stopping kiss.

"Ahhh… now I remember," Ailsa husked when, eventually, they broke for air.

Dinner was a lively affair. Any residual awkwardness had dissipated, supplanted by a conviviality few could have foreseen the night before. It was clear a fledgling romance was budding between Marianne and Liam, although no one was tactless enough to voice a caution that in two days, one would leave with no immediate plans to return.

Lady Travers' relatively unruffled life in London beckoned, and she found her thoughts winging to her husband whom she had missed with an unexpected intensity. It was rare for them to be apart and, while wonderful to spend time with her son, had found aspects of this last two weeks... exacting.

She had forgotten the capricious whims of young ladies, especially when their welfare was your responsibility, grateful her own daughter, once equally flighty, was happily married.

Initially, Delia, who had no mind to draw attention to herself after the previous night's fiasco, tried to blend in with the furnishings. Gently, the others coaxed her into conversation and before long, she was entering into the various debates with verve.

Her natural exuberance, not to mention a canny intelligence, which, until this evening was hidden under a veneer of what Delia believed to be sophistication, revealed a young lady of admirable qualities — and, at least, her faux pas had unfolded miles from the spiteful gossips.

Ignoring one minor, to which the majority of the guests remained oblivious, indiscretion... as house parties went,

Lord Annersleigh's first — and, if he had his way, only — was gauged a resounding success.

Chapter Twenty-Four

Lord Annersleigh's betrothal to Miss Duval was announced by the latter's loving father in front of a packed congregation on Sunday morning, prompting a wave of congratulations from excited well-wishers.

Neither Lewis nor Ailsa was in favour of a protracted engagement but acknowledged they had to allow time for the banns to be read, invitations sent out, and travel arrangements made.

Gervase had suggested a date two months hence, smothering a grin when it was agreed upon with almost indecent celerity.

Monday dawned bright and cold. Whispering Pines hummed with activity as trunks were transferred to coaches, last minute checks made to ensure nothing was forgotten, and, after a hearty breakfast, a flurry of goodbyes said.

Standing a judicious distance from the foot of the stairs to avoid being bundled into a conveyance along with the suitcases, Lewis watched Odin leap onto one of the newel posts, from which vantage point he observed the hustle and bustle with typical disdain.

He walked over to scratch the cat's great grey head, rewarded with an immediate and sonorous purr. "Salutations, my good fellow. I wager you will be glad when the house returns to normal."

Odin blinked slowly and emitted a sound somewhere between a growl and a mewl, which Lewis interpreted as feline for, 'Of course you piffling underling.'

The baize door flew open, and Ailsa appeared, panting a little, her cheeks flushed, and her hair unravelling.

"Did you run all the way?" Lewis smirked.

"I feared I might miss them. I was helping papa and forgot the time." She grinned at him, her green eyes sparkling.

Lewis risked a furtive kiss, wholly unperturbed by the fact that this woman, although breathtakingly beautiful, smart as a whip, and generous to a fault, was also impulsive, a trifle eccentric, and a complete scatterbrain. Their union would be anything but conventional.

He could not wait.

Suddenly, everyone was ready. The manor seemed to deflate as guests and members of the household alike surged outside in a swell of slightly nervous, pre-travel chatter.

Lewis helped his mother into the Travers' Town Coach while Craddock assisted Marianne and Delia. Ailsa, after wishing them Godspeed and promising to write, joined

Lewis. Side by side, they waved goodbye as their guests and their entourage began the long journey home.

The coaches were almost out of sight when Ailsa spotted a blur of movement and her ears discerned the faint thud of hooves.

Shading her eyes with her hand, she squinted. "Lewis, who is that?" Visions of marauding highwaymen on the hunt, scudded though her head. She shuddered, then recalled the drivers, cognisant of the assorted hazards — human or animal — skulking on the roads, were well-armed.

Following her gaze, Lewis stared. The horse with its, thus far indistinct, rider was flying along the track from the village.

"Surely it cannot be someone with ill-intent? Not on a bright and clear Monday morning so close to the manor."

Ailsa looked at Lewis. He nodded, and the pair rushed down the drive.

Three ladies, comfortably ensconced in the first coach, were admiring the vista. Marianne craned her neck to see whether she could catch a last glimpse of the manor.

Over the rumble of the wheels, she heard a shout. Bewildered, and presuming they had left something behind — although, bearing in mind the mountain of luggage wedged into the conveyances, she was at a loss as to what, she leant out of the window.

"Marianne, what on earth are you doing?" Lady Travers tutted. "The last thing we need is an ungainly spill. Sit down."

"Someone is coming," Marianne stayed where she was but twisted to face the speaker. "Has either of you forgotten anything?"

Delia and Lady Travers looked at each other and shook their heads. "No," they chorused.

"Then what…" Marianne trailed off as the rider came into view.

It was Liam.

Her heart raced, skipped a beat, then another before settling into an erratic rhythm. Her hand fluttered to her chest as Liam closed the gap.

"Stop, please stop," she beseeched Mr Rogers, the Travers' driver who, spying the approach of an apparent stranger was inclined to spur on the horses.

Reluctantly he gave a signal, and reined in the six. The fleet of carriages slowed.

"Marianne Fletcher, what has got into you?" Lady Travers admonished, reverting to informality in her shock.

A head appeared at the window.

"Mr Davidson?" Lady Travers did not bother to hide her surprise. "To what do we owe the pleasure?"

"A word with Miss Fletcher, if I may?" he addressed the countess, but his gaze remained locked on Marianne.

"Make it quick. We have many miles to cover before day's end," Lady Travers replied testily and flapped her hand, sinking back against the cushions.

Liam dismounted, opened the door, dropped the step, and offered Marianne his hand.

"It could not be conducted through the window?" Lady Travers snapped, to Delia's swiftly masked amusement. "No, of course it could not. You youngsters, no sense of decorum, or urgency."

Blushing, but determined not to miss a single second with Liam, Marianne gripped his fingers and climbed down, just as Ailsa and Lewis emerged from the shadow of the tree-lined drive.

She bit her lip to prevent a wild giggle from erupting at the varying degrees of astonishment on the faces of those surrounding her.

"Liam." She smiled, embracing this unanticipated extra moment with him, imprinting his arresting features into her mind. "Is something amiss?"

"Yes," he replied, bluntly.

"What? What is wrong?" A sliver of panic rippled through Marianne.

"I cannot let you leave. We have known each other less than three days, mere hours, but the thought of you disappearing from my life is untenable. Please stay."

"L-Liam…" Whatever Marianne thought he was going to say, this took the wind out of her sails. "I must, my home, my family…" even as she spoke, she was entranced by the cerulean blue of his eyes, the unruly forelock falling across his brow, his broad shoulders, muscular chest encased in white shirt under a dark blue jacket… *Marianne control yourself* her rational side adjured. *Elope with him*, her romantic side countered. *My, but you are presumptuous*, logic taunted.

Steadfastly ignoring her inner debate, she tried again. "My family await my return. I live in London. I have no home here and cannot outwear my welcome at the manor."

Ailsa opened her mouth, to have Lewis press her hand in tacit caution. She glanced at him, and he shook his head mouthing, "Wait."

Liam entwined his fingers with Marianne's, his touch eliciting a veritable glissade of thrills to coast down her spine, then dropped onto one knee.

Ailsa's gasp was echoed by Delia and Lady Travers who had alighted from the coach, the latter groaning in disbelief. Her vexed, "What is it with you two? Are you determined to give me apoplexy?" Was heard only by Delia who maintained her serene countenance by sheer effort of will.

Liam spoke with firmness of purpose. "My dearest Miss Fletcher, Marianne. I concede we barely know each other, but whether it be three days or three thousand, my love will never diminish. We are of different status. I cannot offer you the luxuries you deserve which, I am sure, a far more suitable nobleman would bestow upon you, but I can offer you my heart, my soul, and my unwavering devotion. If you dare to take a risk on a humble farmer, I promise to love, honour, and cherish you from now until the day I die."

Marianne gawked — there was no other word to describe her stupefied reaction.

Not naive enough to presume this would be easy — Liam was correct in that their worlds were radically different — Marianne had never been more certain of anything in her entire life. *Precipitous? Yes. Deranged? Quite possibly. Reckless? Definitely.*

Nevertheless...

Marianne was the antithesis of spontaneous. She behaved exactly as the daughter of a viscount ought; never rocked the apple cart, never stepped out of line. Although her head whirled with the implications of her decision, she knew, without question, it was the only one. Moreover, she was less than a month short of her majority and there was no arrangement in place to which she had no alternative but to adhere.

The silence stretched out until Ailsa, forcing herself not to fidget, wanted to scream.

"Humble farmer?" Disentangling her right hand, Marianne cupped Liam's jaw. "Sir, I beg to differ. I confess, I am unsure what it is to be in love but the notion I might never see you again, is like a knife to my heart. To be apart from you for a single moment leaves an ache nothing can assuage. If I was to accept your proposal, how...?" she hesitated.

Sensing there was a decent chance Marianne might just abscond with Liam, Lewis intervened. "If I might be so bold, and before this becomes too complicated, perhaps the solution is a compromise. Miss Fletcher, consider an extension to your visit here, allowing you the opportunity to write to your family and time to discover whether what you feel for Mr Davidson is genuine and enduring."

"Marianne, I simply cannot…" desperately, Lady Travers, knowing she was fighting a losing battle, tried to dissuade… this had disaster written all over it.

"Lady Travers, forgive me. I know this is rash, but it is also my choice, my future. I am not a fool. Trust me."

Lady Travers searched Marianne's face and whatever she saw satisfied her… for now. "You are correct, it is your life, and much as I feel I ought to be the voice of reason, I surmise it will fall on deaf ears," she replied archly. "At least I have a week to compose an explanation for your absence which will not give your mother a fit of the vapours."

"Thank you," Marianne dipped a curtsy, then looked at Lewis. "May I request a sheet of paper to write a note to mama?"

"We shall never get to the coaching inn," Lady Travers bemoaned.

Delia hugged her friend. "Good for you," she murmured. "Faith, but I wish I had your courage."

"Says the lady who wrestled a cat." Marianne gave a carefree laugh, wanton disregard for Society's unwritten *code* making her giddy.

Chapter Twenty-Five

Below a clear sky darkening from a fiery sunset to deep indigo, Whispering Pines seemed to heave a long sigh of relief, and relax on its foundations.

With the departure of the last remaining guests, the household was slowly reverting to its usual sedate pace, embracing the serenity after two weeks of what could only be described as genteel chaos.

Marianne was in her bedchamber, penning an exhaustive letter, praying the recipients would not judge her harshly and understand what had motivated her to risk everything on what would seem to them to be the flimsiest of grounds.

Somewhat of a wallflower, Marianne only attended Society events to oblige her mother, preferring walks in the parks and quiet nights at home with her beloved books to balls and soirees.

Her mother despaired, wondering how her daughter

would ever meet an eligible bachelor, unaware that, until three days ago, Marianne had rarely pondered the notion.

She hoped her parents, who loved each other dearly, despite their own marriage being arranged, understood her reasoning.

If it all fell apart, the only thing she had lost was time.

Wrapped up warmly against the evening air, Lewis, as had become customary was walking Ailsa home. Their chatter, carrying across the stillness, was silenced abruptly and frequently when one decided it was high time they kissed the other... rules be damned.

They came to the top of the gentle rise marking the edge of the estate. Behind them towered Whispering Pines, shrouded in the gloom, the dark façade illuminated here and there by the flickering glow of a candelabra on an unshuttered window ledge.

In front, the higgledy piggledy roofs of Chesmere, along with the comforting hum of people going about their nightly routines. The odd slurred voice drifting towards them, indicating this included those who, after indulging in one beer too many were crawling home from the centuries-old alehouse.

Lewis paused.

The moonrise cast a silvery sheen across the landscape, creating a mystical world of shadows and light. He stared, rapt, Alisa's words coming back to him, *I am certain you will enjoy living here. It gets under your skin, becoming so much a part of you that to walk away would be tantamount to severing a limb,* along with the sensation — the one he had experienced all those months ago — that he was where he was supposed to be.

If given to fancy, Lewis might suspect his uncle had second sight, or the gift of divination. Halstead Thorne had bequeathed more than bricks and mortar, more than a title. Here, in this remote corner of England, to where Lewis had travelled begrudgingly and under duress, his uncle had given him a purpose, a raison d'être and, most importantly, a love without whom he could not imagine taking another step.

Lewis' lips twitched at the irony.

"What is wrong? Does something bother you?" Ailsa's question pierced his reverie.

He squeezed her arm tucked around his. "Nothing at all. In fact, I think for once in my life, everything is exactly right."

"How so?" She faced him, her head canted as she tried to read his expression.

"It occurs to me that my inheritance, although composed on vellum, might just as easily been written in the stars."

Astonished by his lyrical turn of phrase, Ailsa stared at him. "My, my, how poetic. What brought that on? Mayhap your third glass of wine? The brandy?"

"No, you imp. Merely a moment's introspection."

"About the will?"

"More about its effect."

"Would you care to elaborate?"

Lewis corralled his thoughts. "I did not want this." He swung his arm in a wide arc as though encompassing the estate. "I felt Uncle Halstead had foisted it on me as some kind of punishment for a transgression I had no idea I had committed. I have already mentioned it was my mother who convinced me to come, saying something along the lines of what was a year anyway, and if I was recluse in the middle of the city, being a recluse in the middle of nowhere ought to suit me perfectly.

"I had many, *many* reservations, but the slew of emotions and sensations which swamped me upon my arrival demolished every single one, almost instantly. Never has anywhere felt more like home than Whispering Pines, not even the house I grew up in and returned to after the war. It was as unnerving as it was exhilarating.

"Then I met you. I did not recognise it at first, but you were the missing piece — like the last note in a song, or the last word in chapter — without which I would never be whole, and, by some miracle, you reciprocated my affection.

"Of all the people upon whom my uncle could bestow his legacy, he chose me. A nephew he had not seen for over a decade. Why?"

"Perhaps because this, your inheritance, is a state of *mind* not a state of being. More than goods and chattels, however treasured, it is a privilege imbued with memory and history," Ailsa offered quietly.

"It is one thing to read it on a sheet of vellum, quite another to walk the tracks, breathe the air, see the people, the buildings, the livestock. Uncle Thorne discerned you were the one person who would appreciate and continue his legacy.

"Words are naught but an essence. The bond, the sense of kinship develops when the words become tangible. You arrived and it felt like home. The connection was immediate."

As Lewis listened, a line from Hamlet popped into his mind and he quoted almost absently, "There are more things in heaven and earth, Horatio, than are dreamt of in your philosophy."

"You will not hear any argument from me on that score." Ailsa grinned, adding, "On a similar theme, it might interest you to know, Uncle Thorne insisted that — notwithstanding my vehement denials — one day when I least excepted it, a tall dark-haired man would sweep me off my feet. I never took him seriously, yet here we are."

For a long moment, the only sounds were leaves rustling in the trees and the hoot of an owl, as each contemplated the almost impossible odds which brought them together. Had they ignored a single one, their paths might never have crossed.

"Here we are." A trace of awe crept into Lewis' voice. Taking Ailsa in his arms, he looked skywards. "Thank you, Uncle Halstead, for believing a baron's inheritance was so much more than an endowment. You bequeathed me hope, life, and a love immeasurable. I promise to honour your faith in me."

"Lewis," Ailsa was enchanted… *my, but he had a way with words.*

"Yes, my darling."

"Kiss me."

"Nothing would give me greater joy."

Bathed in the celestial glow of the rising moon, Lewis kissed Ailsa into dizzy delirium and, at last, a state of mind became a state of being.

Epilogue

1825
Winter

Immersed in all things estate related, it took several minutes for the peals of merriment to pierce the consciousness of the gentleman absorbed by estate accounts.

Closing the ledger, Lewis Burroughs, 4th Marquis of Chesbrough, rose from his chair and crossed the room to lean against the frame of the great French windows.

He grinned at the sight of three figures frolicking in the snow with joyful abandon, their cheerful shouts carrying on the frigid air. His gaze fell on his wife, as bewitching as the day they met and no less irrepressible — despite her lofty title of marchioness.

Balanced like a statue on the low wall bordering the gardens, a huge grey cat... his plume of a tail ramrod straight... presided over proceedings with feline hauteur.

Shaking his head at the madcap antics of his family, Lewis shrugged into his heavy coat, tied a woollen scarf — a

Christmas gift from Ailsa — around his neck, and opened the doors onto the terrace.

Odin turned at the soft crunch of footsteps on the snow-covered flagstones. His ears pricked up, and he stretched, arching his back in readiness to receive the appropriate degree of adoration due a creature of his exalted status. Reaching the cat, Lewis obliged, burying his rapidly cooling fingers into the soft, velvety fur.

Beneath the wall and unseen from the library, three kittens of indeterminate heritage, although Odin had been looking particularly proud of himself lately, romped under the watchful eye of Ailsa.

"You three… wait," he counted, pointing at everyone, including cats, in turn, "seven… will catch your deaths out here. 'Tis bitter," Lewis exclaimed.

"Come, join us," his wife urged. "We're about to make snow angels."

"Papa, Papa, pleeeeeeeeeeease," Philippa, known to all and sundry as Pippa, his nearly four-year-old — as she kept reminding everyone — daughter chimed in, jigging about in excitement.

"Of course, you are." He rolled his eyes good-humouredly and walked down the broad steps to be met by Elliott, Philippa's twin, who grabbed his hand and dragged him to a patch of pristine whiteness.

"Is this wise?" He met his wife's laughing gaze over the children's heads.

"Not in the slightest." Ailsa giggled. "When has that ever stopped me?"

"Never in my recall," he replied waggling his eyebrows comically. "Come on then, you two rapscallions, show me how to make a snow angel."

With ecstatic squeals, the twins lay flat in the snow, stretched out their arms and legs, then swept them up and down, and out and in, respectively.

"Your turn, Papa." Elliot, liberally besprinkled in snow, jumped up and indicated a spot alongside.

"Must I?" Lewis clutched his head dramatically and pretended to run away.

"Yes, yes," Pippa shrieked, chasing after him and seizing his hand. "'Tis fun. Then a snowman."

Surrendering to the inevitable, Lewis did as beseeched, but deliberately misconstrued their instructions every step of the, very short, way, prompting a lot of *humphs* and *Papa's* from his long-suffering offspring.

Used to this, the twins played along, chortling with glee when the kittens bounced onto their prostrate father, leaving white paw prints all over his dark grey coat.

Spluttering with mirth, Ailsa — who looked like a, rather rumpled, fairy-tale princess with her flame hair spilling out of its neat bun, eyes sparkling, and cheeks pink — reached out a hand to pull Lewis up from the soft powder.

He waved her off. "I can manage." Levering himself upright, Lewis suffered the children dusting, or in their case it was more like beating, him down. "Be careful love, don't over-do it," his tone hushed, for her ears only.

"Trust me," Ailsa smiled at her husband, and, for a split second, there was just the two of them. All other sound faded into the background.

Always in tune with one another, their affinity was currently laced with a touch of wonder. Three weeks previously, she had been informed by the local doctor that her queasiness was nothing to do with an excess of rich fruit cake on Christmas Day, and everything to do with the fact he believed she was increasing.

It was relatively early days, and Lewis was wont to cluck like an anxious hen, which Ailsa, being Ailsa, balked at but loved him the more for it.

Their eyes met, vivid green on tender grey.

Lewis brushed a kiss to Alisa's forehead. "Brrr… I know you are having fun, sweetheart, but if we do not go inside, I fear your delectable nose will freeze and snap off."

Ailsa sniggered. "Fine, if you insist…"

"I do."

"…Elliott, Pippa," she hailed the twins who paused in the middle of throwing fistfuls of snow at each other and, wearing matching expressions of innocence, faced their parents.

Shaking her head fondly, Ailsa schooled her features. "Come along, before we cannot tell you apart from the snowmen. Inside with you. To the back door, and don't forget to stamp your feet to rid your boots of snow and mud."

She scooped up the wriggling kittens, and glanced over her shoulder to see Odin descend from his perch and scoot ahead.

With a great show of reluctance, the two children stomped their way from the garden, around the corner of the house, across the courtyard, and in through the back door, doffing coats, gloves, hats, and scarves as they did, remembering, miracle of miracles, to hang them on the hooks.

Boots were exchanged for slippers, then they scampered to the warmth of the library, followed by their doting parents who apologised to their amused staff for the snowy footprints marring the stone floor.

Shortly thereafter, peace enveloped the room. Philippa was reading one of her favourite books, eyes drooping after charging about in the fresh air, and Elliott was engrossed in a jigsaw puzzle. Odin had made a beeline for his basket near the hearth, and the kittens were snuggled up to their mother in the kitchen.

A steaming cup of hot chocolate warming her hands,

Ailsa sank onto the capacious chaise next to Lewis who tucked her against him and pressed his lips to her bright hair.

"If I had to describe perfection, this might just pass muster," she murmured, nestling into her husband's arms.

"Hmmm… more like the repercussions of acceding to the terms of a will," Lewis said, tongue-in-cheek, and glanced sideways at his wife, in expectation of her huffed riposte.

He did not have to wait long.

"Lewis Burroughs, do not refer to our children as repercussions." Indignantly, Ailsa elbowed him in the ribs.

"So predictable," he teased. "Ooof, no need for violence," when she did it again, "I surrender."

"Humph." Her nose flared and her eyes narrowed suspiciously.

"I promise." He snuck a quick kiss which, he had determined long ago, was the very best way to gain the upper hand in any discussion. Knowing full well his beloved employed the same tactics to her own advantage.

"Lewis," she demurred mildly, "the children."

"Are not looking this way and, returning to your remark… yes, I concur, perfection," Lewis appeased indulgently. "I give you, in all their youthful glory, the baron's inheritance," he declared with deliberate pomposity.

Stifling a giggle, Ailsa sallied, "And the marquis' legacy."

"And Odin's tormentors," Lewis added, straight-faced.

"He loves it. Don't you, poppet?" she cooed.

The object of their discussion raised a bleary eye… *Poppet? Did they not know who he was?* Deciding it was not worth the energy to object, Odin went back to sleep, supremely indifferent to the banter going on around him.

"No sense of occasion," Lewis scoffed.

"There's an occasion?"

"With you, there's always an occasion." He grinned. "Now," he took the cup out of Ailsa's hand and placed it on the adjacent table, "while these two are otherwise occupied, the marquis requires a moment with his marchioness."

"Oh, does he indeed? Lewis, there are children present." Ailsa's token protest was silenced when her husband's lips met hers.

"Hush, my love." He smiled against her mouth.

For once, he got no argument.

In the cosy ambience of the library as snow began to drift down from the laden sky in lazy spirals gradually removing all traces of snow angels, a family settled in for the evening… content in the knowledge the future of Whispering Pines was secure.

About the Author

Rosie Chapel lives in Perth, Australia with her hubby and two furkids. When not writing, she loves catching up with friends, burying herself in a book (or three), discovering the wonders of Western Australia, or — and the best — a quiet evening at home with her husband, enjoying a glass of wine and a movie.

Website: www.rosiechapel.com

Also by Rosie Chapel

<u>Historical Fiction</u>

The Hannah's Heirloom Sequence

The Pomegranate Tree - Book One

Echoes of Stone and Fire - Book Two

Embers of Destiny - Book Three

Etched in Starlight - Prequel

Hannah's Heirloom Trilogy - Compilation — e-book only

Prelude to Fate

Legacy of Flame and Ash

The Nettleby Trilogy (WW1 Novellas)

A Guardian Unexpected - Book One

Under the Clock - Book Two

Between Heartbeats - Book Three

<u>Regency Romances</u>

The Linen and Lace Series

Once Upon An Earl - Book One

To Unlock Her Heart - Book Two

Love on a Winter's Tide - Book Three

A Love Unquenchable - Book Four

A Hidden Rose — Book Five

The Daffodil Garden

The Unconventional Duchess

Rescuing Her Knight - *the de Wiltons:* Book One

Elusive Hearts - *An Unexpected Romance*: Book One

Shrouded Hearts - *An Unexpected Romance*: Book Two

His Fiery Hoyden

A Regency Christmas Double

Fate is Curious

A Christmas Prayer *with Ashlee Shades*

Luck be a Pirate

The Highwayman's Kiss

The Lady's Wager

Winning Emma

A Love Impossible

Unravelling Roana

Love Kindled

Moonbeams and Mistletoe

<u>Fairy Tale Romance</u>

Chasing Bluebells

<u>Contemporary Romances</u>

Of Ruins and Romance

All At Once It's You

Cobweb Dreams

Just One Step

His Heart's Second Sigh

<u>With Rori Bleu</u>

Evie's War

Vindicta

Corrupt Covenant

Lesser of Two Evils

Deadly Incision

Tidbits

The Hunters - Dystopian Fiction

Tapestry of Shadows and Light - Prequel

Echoes & Illusions - Book One

Smoke and Mirrors - Book Two

The Sela Helsdatter Saga

A Flip of The Coin - Book One

Conceived Chaos - Book Two

Odin's Bane - Book Three

Valhalla's Doom - Book Four

Arcane Alchemy - Freya's Fate: A Helsdatter Saga Novella

Butters PI Series

Double Cross

Dereliction of Devotion

Sibling Rivalry

The Mobster's Moll

The Pomegranate Tree

Hannah's Heirloom - Book One

Hoping to trace the origins of an ancient ruby clasp, a gift from her long dead grandmother, Hannah Wilson travels to the fortress of Masada with her best friend, Max.

Strange dreams concerning a rebel ambush begin to haunt Hannah and following a tragic accident, she slips into the world of Ancient Masada.

A woman out of time, Hannah must rely on her instincts and her knowledge of what will befall this citadel to survive.

Will she escape, or is she doomed to die along with hundreds of others as Masada falls — and what does any of this have to do with an ancient ruby clasp?

***

Echoes of Stone and Fire

Hannah's Heirloom - Book Two

Pompeii - a vibrant city lost in time following the AD79 eruption of Vesuvius. Now rediscovered, archaeologists yearn for an opportunity to uncover the town's past.

Some things, however, are best left alone - revealing the secrets hidden beneath the stones could prove perilous.

Hannah and Max are brought to Pompeii by a surprise invitation to join an excavation team who are trying to uncover the city's long history.

After entering an excavated house that bears a Hebrew inscription, Hannah's two worlds collide, and she falls back through time to ancient Pompeii. A place where her ancestor is a physician to gladiators engaged in mortal combat, where riotous mobs run amok and where a ghost from the past returns to haunt her.

Will Hannah and her loved ones manage to escape the devastation she knows is coming, before the town is engulfed in volcanic ash? Will she ever find her way back to Max the love of her life, waiting not so patiently millennia away?

Or will echoes be all that remain?

***

Embers of Destiny

Hannah's Heirloom - Book Three

AD80 - Hannah and Maxentius must embark on a new journey to Northern Britannia.

This harsh frontier is far from the comforts of Rome and danger lurks where least expected; a garrison of soldiers, some unhappy with their isolated posting; local tribes, outwardly accepting of their Roman occupier, but who may still resent the seizure of their lands.

Millennia away, Hannah Vallier finds a familiar item while working in a museum near Hadrian's Wall. It is the pomegranate; carved by Maxentius on Masada. Before Hannah can discuss it with Max, disaster strikes!

Believing her husband has been killed, Hannah retreats into the past, her soul melding with that of her ancestor, but with little idea of what they could face. Is the risk from the conquered tribes, or much closer to home?

As rebellion threatens to shatter a fragile peace, Hannah's heart whispers that just maybe Max isn't dead and that he is calling her home.

Can she trust her heart, or will she remain caught out of time, her destiny floating away like embers on a breeze?

***

Etched in Starlight

Hannah's Heirloom - Prequel

Maxentius - a Roman soldier fresh from the battlefields of Armenia, arrives to take command of the military outpost of Masada, Herod's isolated citadel in the Judaean desert.

A seemingly mundane posting after years of warfare, Maxentius finds it more challenging to maintain a focused garrison than to face the wrath of the Parthians across a disputed frontier.

Hannah - a young Hebrew physician spends her days dealing with injuries from street brawls, deprivation, disease and loss. As her beloved Jerusalem plunges into chaos, her brother — who belongs to a band of rebels determined to drive out their Roman occupiers — tells her of their plans to storm a desert fortress and steal the weapons stored there, persuading his reluctant sister to go with him.

Masada - following the ambush, Hannah finds and treats three badly wounded Roman soldiers. In the aftermath and against impossible odds, Hannah and Maxentius realise that they are more than healer and captive, their fate already etched in starlight.

Prelude to Fate

For Lucia, staring into the jaws of an horrific death, escape seems impossible.

Rufius Atellus, a veteran Roman soldier, is appalled when he recognises one of the victims about to be executed. Surely this is a ghastly mistake?

A ferocious she-wolf, anticipating a tasty meal, suddenly finds herself under a human's control.

In an unexpected twist, and as danger threatens, the lives of all three become inextricably entwined.

Was it chance brought them together in that theatre of bloodshed,
or simply a prelude to fate?

Legacy of Flame and Ash

A Hannah's Heirloom Story

An unremarkable family ring — lost when its owner was killed in
the catastrophic eruption of Vesuvius — is excavated after nearly
two millennia buried under tons of pumice and ash, setting off an
extraordinary sequence of events.

A brazen robbery, and the ring is lost again. The theft and
subsequent investigation, inspire twelve-year-old Cristiano Rossi to
dedicate his life to the search and recovery of stolen artefacts.

Fast forward twenty years. Whispers of a rare item being offered for
sale on the black market, initiates a joint operation between the
Italian and British branches of the, colloquially named, Art Squad.

Hannah Vallier and her tech savvy assistant, Bryony Emerson —
whose abilities to track down the untraceable, led to them assisting
the UK Art and Antiquities Unit — have unearthed an intriguing
thread.

Reluctantly, Cristiano agrees to team up with the pair to thwart the
traffickers, retrieve the artefact and, hopefully, dismantle the site.

What ought to be a routine assignment is complicated by a rogue
operative, an unexpected romance, an ancient connection, and a
very angry ghost!

The Nettleby Trilogy

A Guardian Unexpected

Book One

August 1914: Europe is on the brink of catastrophe. In a small village in rural Lincolnshire, a wife kisses her husband goodbye.

Childhood sweethearts, Eliza and Joe have only been married two years. They could not have imagined how soon they would be torn apart by war, nor that the most unexpected of guardians would offer them hope during their darkest hours.

***

Under the Clock

Book Two

England 1908: Under the clock, on a sleepy station platform nestled in rural Lincolnshire, an unexpected romance blossoms.

Maisie: Every Friday, at precisely five to six, a handsome young man arrives at the station. I know the time because I can see the clock. The train pulls in, punctual as always, and among the alighting passengers is an elderly gentleman. The young man greets him with a smile and a handshake, then tucks his arm through the older man's and they leave the platform.

Every Friday.

Occasionally, we exchange a glance or two and, to be fair, I suspect I notice him more than he notices me.

Fred: I count the hours until Friday afternoon comes around. Not only because this marks the start of the weekend but also, and more importantly, I get to see the flower girl. I am clueless as to her name, yet my heart begins to race the minute the station comes into view. I almost run up the steps onto the platform, hoping for a glimpse of her bright smile.

Every Friday.

I doubt she ever notices me. I'm just a village lad, one more faceless person in the throng.

Then again, you never know what might happen… in an innocuous corner of a quiet platform…

…under the clock

***

Between Heartbeats

Book Three

1916 — France

Polly

Nothing in my training, nor the numerous lectures I endured prior to leaving England prepared me for the horror that is trench warfare.

Assigned to a Field Ambulance — a sneeze away from the front line — the atrocities I witnessed were confronting, harrowing, and a constant challenge to my faith in humanity, yet the experience proved to be endlessly rewarding.

Not content with nursing, the principle reason I volunteered was to drive ambulances. My colleagues, preferring the relative safety of the wards, thought me addled, but I was not to be thwarted, despite the dangers. Saving lives outweighed the fear of being blown up or shot.

The last thing I expected to find in the midst of flying shrapnel was love.

Thad

Two long years with no end in sight; the oft repeated, 'we'll be home by Christmas' — a long-forgotten dream, supplanted by the ceaseless thunder of artillery, acres of mud, collapsing trenches, and the all-pervading stench of death.

A nightmare tempered when the driver of the ambulance dispatched to collect Fred, after his brush with a sniper, turned out to be Polly Armstrong, friend of Fred's wife, Maisie.

The initial shock of recognition morphs into something else; something both tantalising and terrifying.

Anyone with an ounce of common sense would quash such frivolous nonsense; we were in the middle of a battle zone. Clearly, common sense had abandoned me.

Against the odds, in the chaos and confusion of war, romance blossoms but tomorrow is not guaranteed. In that split second between heartbeats, their happily ever after could be snatched away.

Regency Romance

Once Upon An Earl

Linen and Lace - Book One

When Fate saw fit to intervene in the life of Giles Trevallier, the very respectable Earl of Winchester, by dropping a female — soaked to the skin and with no memory of who she is or how she came to be there — literally at his feet, no one could have predicted the outcome.

While uncovering her identity, Giles realises he is falling hopelessly in love with his mystery guest, who unbeknownst to him, is succumbing to similar emotions; but, when the heart is involved, a thoughtless word or gesture can thwart even Fate's best-laid plans.

Faced with misunderstandings, whispers of scandal, secret documents and foreign agents, their chance at a happy ever after seems elusive, but fairy tales often happen when least expected, and love — however inconvenient — usually finds a way to conquer all.

***

To Unlock Her Heart

Linen and Lace - Book Two

Abused by a duke, and shunned by Society, relief seems at hand when Grace Aldeburgh is bequeathed a house in a small village, far from malicious gossips.

Once there, a tentative friendship blooms between Grace and Theo Elliott, the local doctor, who has already resolved to be the man to unlock her heart.

Just when happiness appears to be within her grasp, her erstwhile tormentor once again stalks Grace. After a failed kidnap attempt, the duke's quest culminates in an acrimonious confrontation, and the reason for his venal pursuit becomes agonisingly clear.

***

Love on a Winter's Tide

Linen and Lace - Book Three

Every day, Helena disappears into a world few acknowledge, helping the poor, downtrodden, and abused. A husband is the last thing she can be bothered with.

Busy managing his shipping line, Hugh Drummond sees no need for a wife, whose only joy is dancing and frivolity. If — and it was a huge if — he ever married, it would be to a woman as capable as he, not some giddy society Miss.

Then, Hugh meets Helena and despite their resolve, fate, it seems, has other ideas. As their attraction deepens however, treachery threatens to tear them apart. Will they uncover the perpetrator in time, or will their love be swept away, lost forever on a winter's tide?

***

A Love Unquenchable

Linen and Lace - Book Four

Jessica Drummond, a bright and cheerful young woman, rarely gives romance, let alone love, a thought. Long hours working in her brother's shipping office affords little chance of her ever meeting an eligible bachelor.

Duncan Barrington, veteran of the Napoleonic Wars, believes himself wounded in both body and soul. He has no intention of inflicting his demons on anyone, certainly not a beautiful and, in his opinion, irresponsible city lady.

One cold and snowy morning, the plight of a bedraggled puppy throws Jessica and Duncan together and, as a spark of something indefinable yet wholly unquenchable begins to burn, it is unclear who rescued whom.

***

A Hidden Rose

Linen and Lace - Book Five

After witnessing his mother's grief at the loss of his father, Nick Drummond resolved never to cause someone he loved such distress. Even the happiness of his siblings would not sway him — until he met Rose.

Rose Archer was almost content assisting her doctor father in a tiny fishing village in the north of Yorkshire. To experience the world beyond, a tantalising dream — until she met Nick.

Unexpectedly, the impossible becomes possible, and the renounced — desired above all things, but the shipwreck that brought them together, may yet tear them apart. Will Nick learn to trust his heart, or will his love for Rose remain forever hidden

The Daffodil Garden

Horrifically scarred during the war, William Harcourt - Marquis of Blackthorne - prefers to spend his days in the quiet of his daffodil garden; plants do not pity, turn away, or judge.

Lucy Truscott, whose life is far removed from that of the *ton*, has no idea that by saving the life of a young woman, to whom she bears an uncanny resemblance, her own will be placed in mortal danger.

A chance encounter leads to something more. William begins to trust that Lucy sees the man beneath the scars, while Lucy is persuaded that love might actually transcend status.

Unfortunately, before their courtship has really begun, someone has every intention of ending it - permanently.

The Unconventional Duchess

Refusing to suffer the humiliation of her husband flaunting his mistress at Society events, the newly married Duchess of Wallingstead, Ella Lennox, takes control of her life. She leaves London for the family's country seat in remote Yorkshire.

A woman alone, Ella spends the next four years turning a cold, grim house into a home, and transforming the fortunes of the estate. Not afraid of hard work, she soon earns the respect of those around her with her determination and unconventional attitude.

Out of the blue, the duke arrives. Resigned to another arduous visit, Ella is stunned when it seems he is attempting to court her.

Impossible!

Could her dream of a happy marriage be about to come true?

Everything hangs on a snowstorm, a herd of cows and an uninvited guest!

Rescuing Her Knight

The *de Wiltons* — Book One

A story, invented to keep a little girl distracted, marks the beginning of another tale. One destined to remain unfinished for twenty years.

At thirteen, Adam Marchmain became Kitty de Wilton's 'Knight of the Garden' — a title bestowed following an accident which resulted in six-year-old Kitty having her knee sutured. Kitty never forgot his gallantry, but pledges made as children rarely survive into adulthood.

Their paths separated until Fate decreed, they meet again.

Widowed, badly disfigured and his sight ruined, Adam returns to his family home, a shadow of his former self.

Similarly afflicted, although her scars are invisible, Kitty — against her better judgement — is persuaded to help Adam banish his demons. This requires a subterfuge which, if discovered, might shatter more than the bonds of friendship forged two decades previously.

To Kitty, determined to break through the shield Adam has erected, the risk is worth it.

To see his smile and hear his laughter.

To rescue the knight of her childhood.

Just when a fairy tale ending is within her grasp, Kitty is threatened by the man who murdered her husband. In a cruel twist the tables are turned, and Kitty is the one who needs rescuing.

Elusive Hearts

An Unexpected Romance — Book One

What happens when two people whose elusive hearts fight an indefinable attraction, neither looked for nor desired, dare to dream?

When her fiancé and sister abscond to Gretna Green on her wedding day, Sapphira Beresford longs to escape, to avoid the gossipmongers gloating over her misfortune. Disillusioned, she is determined not to be burnt again, swearing off romance and marriage.

A fortuitous invitation sees her embarking on a journey to Pompeii where she meets Leofwin Colleville, reclusive marquis, amateur antiquarian, and her host for the duration.

Although enamoured of the ruins gradually being unearthed and ecstatic to have the opportunity to assist, Sapphira is troubled by her host's attitude, which blows hot and cold.

A confirmed bachelor, Leofwin Colleville is happiest surrounded by ancient ruins, and would prefer to brave the whole of Napoleon's armies alone, than face a lady on the hunt for a husband. The arrival of an unexpected guest throws his unencumbered existence into turmoil, but the harder he strives to maintain his distance, the more she gets under his skin.

Sparks fly and, as Leofwin's truculence undermines Sapphira's already battered confidence, her adventure of a lifetime seems doomed to disaster.

Until the day she runs afoul of greedy treasure hunters.

In the aftermath what was scorned becomes the one thing they crave above all else, but when it comes to the heart, nothing is ever simple.

***

Shrouded Hearts

An Unexpected Romance - Book Two

For the sin committed...

When the unexpected death of her much older husband, frees Madeline Galleron from a seemingly inescapable nightmare, she decides, as a way to regain her self-respect, that a little retribution is in order.

Working for Lucas Withers, Wolfstan Colleville, the Viscount Carnforth, finds himself assigned to a curious case of blackmail. One which involves, of all things, a dead rose, a poem and, at least, two victims.

Wolfstan's investigation leads him to an unlikely culprit and, as an entirely new plan is concocted, emotions believed forever vanquished are kindled.

A spirited woman, Madeline refuses to let her past dictate her future... *but...* to conquer her torment and take a chance on love, is a whole other matter. Dare she trust Wolfstan to be an honourable man with no ulterior motive? *Could* he be her knight in shining armour?

Can she open her heart, or will it remain forever shrouded?

His Fiery Hoyden

A Novella

Livvy has no respect for the nobility; they let her down when she most needed them. Why should she accede to their demands now?

Philip, Lord Harrington, is stunned to discover the young heir to the dukedom lives a stone's throw away in a ramshackle cottage, and resolves to restore the child to his birthright.

They meet in a clash of wills, but just when it seems Livvy might surrender, the victory Philip desires, may not taste all that sweet.

A Regency Duet

Luck be a Pirate

Luck wasn't something retired pirate Kennet Alexson believed in — good or bad. However, even he had to concede that landing a job at Trentams shipyard, and meeting Lynette Collins, was more than coincidence.

Fortune it seemed, was smiling on him for once.

As Kennet adjusts to life on dry land, his friendship with Lynette deepens into something far more enduring, and what once seemed elusive now becomes possible.

Unfortunately, fate has other plans, and Kennet's good luck is about to run out.

***

The Highwayman's Kiss

Surrendered Hearts — Book One

Nothing exciting had ever happened to Juliette St Clair.

Her days were spent assisting her father or calling on friends, wandering art galleries, taking constitutionals or, and more preferably, escaping into her books. Her evenings her evenings — an endless round of balls, where she preferred to remain invisible.

Until the day she was robbed by a highwayman.

A Regency Christmas Double

Heart Rescued

Four years since Jasper lost the woman he was hoping to marry. Four years since he closed his heart and withdrew from Society. He has no idea his reclusive existence is about to be shattered.

Enter his sister's best friend, Harriet, a flame haired beauty, who needs his help.

Reluctantly he agrees and as they spend time together, it is clear their feelings run deep. Although Harriet affects Jasper in a way no woman ever has, he believes her to be out of his league ~ but it's Christmas and she might just be the one to melt his frozen heart

***

Catch a Snowflake

Romance often blossoms in the most unlikely of places - but in a ward full of wounded soldiers - surely not?

When Lucas Withers comes face to face with Jemima Parsons - a young woman who blames him for her brother's injury - falling in love is the last thing on their minds. What neither of them anticipated, was the magic of snowflakes.

Fate is Curious

A Novella

Happily, ever after? No such thing! Bereft, following her beloved husband's sudden death, Lady Charlotte Sherbrooke has lost her belief in romantic nonsense.

Successful shipping merchant, Zacharie Romain, is no stranger to loss; his business can be hazardous. Moreover, his wife died in childbirth and even though it happened a decade ago, he has no mind to expose himself to such sorrow again.

They meet in less than joyful circumstances but, as the year turns and grief diminishes, the woes of a small boy become the catalyst for something wholly unexpected. Can Charlotte and Zacharie trust what Fate has in store or will past heartbreak prevent them from taking a chance on love?

A Christmas Prayer

with Ashlee Shades

A Short Story

An entreaty from a frightened child.

Orphaned and only nine, Caroline Thorne has to grow up before her time. She is doing everything she can to keep what is left of her family together and out of the workhouse but is terrified her prayers are not being heard. Or maybe they are…

A petition from a woman desperate for a family.

A chance meeting with three orphaned siblings, tugs at Elizabeth Barrington's heart strings. Thus far, she and her husband have not been blessed with children and, as Christmas approaches, a plan begins to form - one which might just be the answer to her prayers.

Two Christmas prayers, as different as they are the same.

Will they hear and, more importantly, heed the answer?

The Lady's Wager

Surrendered Hearts - Book Two

A Novelette

Ged Mowbray will do anything to avoid being married off to the suitable prospects his parents insist on parading in front of him.

Melissa Bouchard is under no illusion her sizeable dowry is the attraction to suitors, not her.

An overheard conversation leads to an offer too good to refuse, but what happens when a lady's wager, becomes a gamble on the happily ever after, you did not even realise you wanted?

***

Winning Emma

Surrendered Hearts - Book Three

A Novelette

Randolph Craythorpe — earl, covert operative, and occasional highwayman — believed his dalliance with Lady Felicity Hartwich would lead to marriage. It did, but not to him! The arrival of an unwelcome guest, however, provides the perfect opportunity to indulge in a little retaliation.

Emma Newbury accompanies her cousin, Lady Charity Anscombe, to London for the Christmas season. Once there, she comes face to face with the three men who witnessed the humiliating aftermath of her father's disgrace — one of whom, to her irritation, has taken up residence in her dreams.

Their infrequent encounters only serve to confuse but, while winter tightens its grip on the city, what was inconceivable becomes the

one thing for which they both yearn, yet bound by Society's rules,
cannot admit.

As the snow falls, Randolph begins to understand that to win Emma,
he will have to surrender.

***

Moonbeams and Mistletoe

Surrendered Hearts - Book Four

A Novelette

*If we are part of a universe where moonbeams and mistletoe exist, nothing
is insurmountable for, otherwise, what is the point?*

To Emily Livingston, spinster — this deceptively frivolous phrase
was all she had left of her betrothed.

To Henry Bartholomew, widower — the sentiment, while naïve, also
serves as a reminder that even in the darkest of hours, light can be
found… it was simply a matter of perspective.

When four-year-old twins run into Emily — literally — she has no
idea where their unexpected encounter will lead. Determined to
ensure his children are *not* being schooled into something nefarious,
Henry resolves to meet this mysterious lady who has enthralled the
duo with her stories.

One dull and otherwise ordinary autumnal morning, two disparate
souls are brought together, and long-forgotten emotions are stirred.

The question is whether Henry and Emily have the courage to
follow their hearts or be forever trapped in the sadness of the past.
Can moonbeams and mistletoe persuade them, the answer was
there all along?

A Love Impossible

A Regency M/M Novelette

Tasked with investigating a heinous crime, Edward Lindsay travels from London to Dublin — a city which holds too many memories — in the guise of guardian to his sister. He knew it could be hazardous, and relished the challenge, but that wasn't what caused his stomach to tighten as they approached landfall.

Dublin held more than just a murderer.

There was also Aidan.

While attending a party, Aidan Griffen is astonished when he comes face to face with a man who fled Dublin two years previously. A man he has desperately tried to forget.

As Edward closes in on his quarry, a fire, deliberately extinguished, is rekindled. But what of it? Edward and Aidan share a love impossible, and to acknowledge their feelings — more dangerous than confronting a killer.

Is there any hope of a happily ever after?

Unravelling Roana

A Regency Novelette

Tired of being ignored by her husband, Roana Dumont, Countess of Brooketon does the one thing guaranteed to get his attention. She runs away… to Venice, leaving behind a set of riddles for him to solve… *if* he feels their marriage is worth saving.

Gideon Dumont, 6th Earl of Brooketon is flabbergasted when he discovers his wife has apparently vanished off the face of the earth. A series of puzzles, the only clue as to her whereabouts.

The question is… will he unravel them?

Love Kindled

A Regency Novelette

Recently widowed, Amelia Ingram - Countess of Gresham, decides to shake off the fetters from her arranged and loveless marriage. Exploiting her new-found independence, Amelia indulges her yearning to explore - incognito.

Her ploy works so well, she receives an offer of employment from the dangerously handsome, Rupert Latimer - Earl of Badlesmere. On impulse, she accepts and finds herself governess to Cate, a delightful scamp of a child. What began as a bit of a game on Amelia's part, evolves into something far more profound, and a flame she presumed impossible to ignite, is kindled.

An unexpected turn of events leads to yet another offer. This time there is far more at stake and, determined history not repeat itself, Amelia confesses her ruse.

Rupert has been burnt once. Will he douse the spark, or take a risk and trust his heart?

Fairy Tale Romance

Chasing Bluebells

A Fairy Tale Novella

Once upon a time, somewhere in France, there was a man whose reckless obsession led him down a dark path — one which, ultimately, cost him his life.

That ought to have been the end of it.

Regrettably, as is so often the case, those who least deserve it, suffer for the actions of others.

A decade after being sent away, Sebastien Daviau returns to the little village where everything began. Hoping to lay the ghosts of his childhood to rest, he studiously ignores the possibility, he might run into Charlotte de Montbeliard.

As luck would have it, Charlotte is the one who runs into him… well, his horse… and although the brief encounter leaves a lasting impression, neither recognises the other.

A name revealed causes a freak accident, catapulting Sebastien's past into his present, and bringing him face to face with a man whose reputation would intimidate the most ardent of suitors.

Can whatever is blossoming between Charlotte and Sebastien survive the challenge imposed, or is their happily ever after about to fade as quickly as the bluebells they loved to chase?

Of Ruins and Romance

Kassandra Winters has intrigued Gabriel St Germain since he accidentally knocked her flying outside her university professor's office. Her face haunts his dreams, yet he never expected to see her again. So, he is surprised when she appears, as though destined to do so, in the middle of a ruin, and he concocts a plan to win her heart.

Gabriel's old-fashioned courtship touches something deep inside Kassie and, although struggling to believe someone as handsome as Gabriel could possibly be interested in her, she soon realises she has fallen irrevocably in love with him. However, just as Kassie shares everything of herself with Gabriel, her world comes crashing down.

Can their romance survive, or will it fall in ruins, like the relics of antiquity that brought them together?

All At Once It's You

When Alex arrives in the small village of Rosedale Abbey, to take up a position as a research assistant for a renowned archaeologist, the last thing she is looking for, or expects to find, is love.

Jake was perfectly happy with the status quo. When it came to relationships, he didn't do committed or long term. He called the shots, and if his current flame didn't like it, she knew what to do. A philosophy, which served him well - until he met Alex.

Romance blooms, but even as the untamed wilderness of the North Yorkshire moors weaves its spell, a long-buried secret might yet jeopardise their happily ever after.

Cobweb Dreams

A Novella

A holiday on the Scottish isle of Mull was just the break Chloe Shepherd needed, an escape from her boring office job and her complete lack of anything resembling a social life. Romance, it seems, isn't on the cards and, although Chloe dreams of finding her soulmate she is beginning to believe love is like cobwebs — spun overnight, only to vanish in the early morning breeze.

Under sufferance, Dominic Winters makes a flying visit to Mull to check on a rental property owned by his family. He hasn't got time for this — so indulging in a holiday fling is the last thing on his mind.

A lamb stuck in a bog proves a most unexpected matchmaker and, while Mull weaves its magic, Chloe wonders whether those fragile cobwebs might be far more stubborn than she thought.

Just One Step

A Short Story

In the aftermath of an horrific car accident, Daisy Forrester travels to Italy - hoping, so far from her memories, she might begin to heal.

Archaeologist, and single father, Adam Willoughby is too busy looking after his young daughter to give romance let alone love, a thought.

Neither expects a chance encounter in an ancient ruin to be anything more, but sometimes, that's all it takes.

His Heart's Second Sigh

A Novella

Reuben Faulkner and Paige Latimer are two happily single people, who have no desire to upset the status quo.

Unexpectedly, they are thrown together, only to discover both want far more than a casual friendship.

Just when things take an interesting turn, Reuben's past catches up with them, and threatens to derail their blossoming romance before it has chance to start.

With Rori Bleu

Evie's War

World War II catapulted ordinary people into extraordinary service to save the world from an insidious evil... even if that meant being forced to do things which, under normal circumstances, would be considered abhorrent.

Genevieve Rousseau, Evie to a select few, was one such person who could not escape this fate. Despite her covert endeavours to liberate Paris from the Germans, she finds herself labelled a collaborator and an enemy of the French Republic.

Her only hope of vindication lies in helping a dangerously handsome American, with questionable motives, to uncover the Germans' final revenge.

Could struggling to resist Major Jack Donovon prove to be the decisive battle in Evie's War?

Vindicta

Nightmares come in many guises… but usually fade with the dawn…

Not so for Bobbi Jo Fletcher. A witness to the massacre of her family, she had to escape the murderers in the middle of the worst blizzard in centuries… and she was only 5!

Fast forward twelve years and Bobbi Jo dreams of starting a new life away from the trauma of her past and the antipathy of pitiless relatives.

The nightmare isn't over… but perhaps the tables have turned…

Vindicta - when death isn't retribution enough…

Corrupt Covenant

A pledge of eternal peace and prosperity sounds too good to refuse… unless, of course, the pledge comes from an immortal dragon.

A contract established in exchange for a king's life and the protection of his lineage should have expired when a desperate queen, facing hordes baying for her destruction, loses faith in the oath… but evil has a long memory.

Trapped for a millennium in a sarcophagus at the bottom of the Danube, death lay beyond the queen's grasp until the day nature, fate, and a mysterious archaeologist joined forces to dredge her from her grave.

A life revived. A liegeman doomed to be reborn until he saves his queen. A dragon who has not forgiven an act of betrayal.

Can two souls, separated for a millennium, break the corrupt covenant, or are they fated to dance to the dragon's tune, for eternity?

The Hunters - Dystopian Fiction

Tapestry of Shadows and Light - Prequel

At the end of civilisation what remains?

Amidst death and destruction, Noemi Ricci struggles to protect her two daughters and escape the encroaching nightmare. It is an uphill battle, but Noemi refuses to let Fate determine her future, and sets out to forge her own destiny.

In a fractured world of shadows and light, it takes every ounce of Noemi's courage and wit to the survive the silent killer stalking humanity, and keep her family together.

Is there any hope of restoring the once beautiful tapestry of life, or will the wrath of Mother Nature destroy it for ever?

***

Echoes & Illusions - Book 1

Twenty years after a global plague, the remnants of civilisation struggle to eke out an existence in a world where humanity is secondary to survival.

On the outskirts of a once vibrant Rome, Gabriel tends his vineyard. From dawn to dusk, he strives to carve out a living, while caring for Bianca, his heavily pregnant wife.

Life might be tough, but at least he had an income, meagre though it was. Trouble seemed a distant memory, until the day he notices their neighbours are not at work in the adjacent fields.

A gruesome discovery sparks a chain of events to rival the conflicts Rome witnessed at the height of its power. Gabriel and Bianca must pit their wits and their lives against a formidable opponent, in an attempt prevent an atrocity none could have predicted.

A bond, forged in a snowy field and strengthened in a city under siege, is put to the ultimate test.

In a world of echoes and illusions, is their love strong enough to surmount the odds, or will it crumble to dust like the empire their enemies are striving to replicate?

***

Smoke & Mirrors - Book 2

In the aftermath of their fiery clash, an uneasy truce forged between

Sophia's Hunters and the Dwellers of Rome allowed life to resume its relatively untroubled rhythm... almost...

... but history warns, it is never a good idea to become complacent.

To the north, a new nightmare materialises. Supported by a band of vindictive acolytes, Carlyle Worthington, the self-proclaimed Pope of Bologna, is determined bring the disparate territories of Italy under his authority and has no hesitation in neutralising anyone who dare thwart his ambition.

As the winds of destruction gain momentum, is the fragile accord strong enough to unite the erstwhile enemies against a common foe, or will the Pope divide and conquer?

Can the fledgling alliance crush the insidious advance, and expose Worthington's fear mongering as little more than smoke and mirrors before evil prevails?

The Sela Helsdatter Saga

A Flip of the Coin - Book One

What happens in Helheim *never* stays in Helheim.

Sela Helsdatter wishes it would. Punished for allowing her quest for power to rule her actions, she has endured eons of torment.

The flip of a coin seems to offer some hope of redemption but, tasked with ridding the world of her erstwhile captor and lover, escape does not mean freedom.

No problem for a warrior queen... right?

Wrong!

Sela is no longer in ninth century Norðvegr, but twenty-first century New York with all its challenges, and where slightest misstep could spell her doom.

Aided by the most unlikely hero, Sela scours the city for her adversary, who delights in taunting her, determined to drag her back to Hell.

Will she prevail, or will A Flip of the Coin catapult her back to the abyss?

***

Conceived Chaos - Book Two

After ridding the world of her tormentor, and finding the love of her life, Sela Helsdatter could be forgiven for thinking she deserves a little peace.

No such luck!

Marriage to the God of Mischief is a walk in the park compared with the terror about to be unleashed from Valhalla. A diabolical edict from Odin himself sees the nine months pregnant, Sela fleeing from the entire Norse pantheon — with no clue why.

A price on her head and a target on her belly, the only person she can trust is her husband, who is keeping her in the dark.

Does her unborn child hold the key to this Conceived Chaos?

***

Odin's Bane - Book Three

Sela Helsdatter cannot catch a break. Relentless in his jealousy and wrath, Odin is determined that neither Sela nor her infant daughter will survive.

Shattered by loss, and with no time to grieve, Sela has to rely on the one person she believes responsible for her current predicament.

A lost friendship revived, the disparate trio seek refuge in a remote corner of Montana, with the uneasy awareness the child may be the key to their salvation.

Vowing Odin will not harm a hair on her daughter's head, Sela has to use every trick at her disposal to thwart the Norse Deity. At the

same time another fiendish subversion threatens the future of
humanity.

Will Odin be victorious… or is another power stirring which will
prove to be his bane?

***

Valhalla's Doom - Book Four

The obsidian stone with its strange steak of neon blue, hanging on a
gold chain around Anna Helsdatter's neck — forged from the
magma surrounding Jörmungandr's cave — serves as a reminder of
the last terrible battle against an insidious evil. The day, Anna came
into her full power to defeat the All Father when he sought to
destroy not only her family, but also every one of the Nine Realms.

A stone which, unbeknownst to Anna — currently contending with
an even greater challenge, that of being college student — hides its
own secret.

Putting her past behind her and, despite contending with a family
composed of the most powerful deities on Earth or in Valhalla, all
Anna wants to do, is to enjoy being a normal nineteen-year-old.

Then again, things involving the Helsdatters, are anything but
normal, and Anna is catapulted into another life-or-death struggle.
The only problem is, this time the stakes are higher… and one
wrong move could spell disaster — especially when saving Earth,
might herald Valhalla's Doom.

Just your typical rock and hard place!

***

Arcane Alchemy

Freya's Fate

A Helsdatter Sage Novella

What happens when the goddess of seduction and love finds herself
on the losing end of a romance…to a human no less? She packs up,

summons her carriage, and sets off to unravel a mystery which has intrigued her for eons.

Where are the deities of this realm? Have they fallen to their doom, never to be revived?

Freya's odyssey takes her to far-flung temples, ancient ruins, and bustling cities, but she is no closer to resolving the riddle, until she arrives in Dublin. In a land where myth and legend are interwoven with everyday life, Freya teeters on the brink of achieving her goal *and* her happily ever after, only to flee to the very couple who triggered her quest.

An unexpected discovery spurs a repeat performance but, this time, Freya no longer cares about the answer. As far as she is concerned, every last god deserves to be consigned to oblivion.

All she wants is to find peace.

Once again, it hovers… tantalisingly close.

Only to be snatched away...

…for Freya's fate is inextricably linked to the one person she is determined to avoid and, to ignore the not-so-subtle summons for help will lead to tragedy.

Some deities have not vanished, some prowl on the periphery preparing to pounce and, as ever when gods interfere in the lives of mortals, chaos ensues.

It will take more than a touch of arcane alchemy to avert the looming catastrophe.

Lesser of Two Evils

If you ask the average American who they intend to vote for in the next election, inevitably, and almost predictably, their reply will be… THE LESSER OF THE TWO EVILS.

Usually, things even out and saner heads prevail… but what happens when the sitting president tries to tip the scales too far in his narcissistic favor simply to get re-elected?

As the world teeters on the brink of a grim fate, it is up to a lone reporter to prevent that from happening…and to stay alive.

Deadly Incision

From the learned halls of the London Hospital to the squalid, bustling streets of Whitechapel surrounding it, life and death walk hand in glove with one another.

This, somewhat fatalistic, status quo was shattered in the autumn of 1888, when Jack the Ripper prowled the darkness, perfecting his 'skills' on unsuspecting women of the night.

Follow us down these same dark and deadly alleyways to hidden corners and stairwells, stained with blood by the legendary Leather Apron's blade to discover a new twist to his story.

Tidbits

A Fictional Miscellany

Can we tempt you to dive into a collection of stories where death prowls in the shadows waiting to pounce?

From a saloon owner, intent on revenge, to a rookie witch, hell-bent on summoning up her dead ancestor. From alien tax dodgers, and hapless bandits, to the horror of WW1.

Hang on to your hats, as we careen from the dusty streets of the lawless wild west to small town… slightly more law abiding but, seemingly, no less dangerous… West Virginia. Take a breath as you are catapulted far beyond our galaxy only to bounce back to earth to witness a bungled bank robbery, before skidding to an ungainly halt in a muddy trench on the edge of no man's land.

At first glance, there is no connection between these disparate tidbits with their colourful characters, until you grasp the common thread – that Death never takes a holiday!

Five tasty morsels – dare you risk a bite?